Cinco De Die-O

Cinco De Die-O

Toni Draper

Desert Palm Press

Cinco De Die-O

(A Paige Turner/Bobbi Garza Mystery – Book 1)

By Toni Draper

©2022 Toni Draper

ISBN (trade) 9781948327619
ISBN (epub) 9781948327909

Desert Palm Press
1961 Main Street, Suite 220
Watsonville, California 95076
www.desertpalmpress.com

Editor: CK King
Cover Design: Michele Bordeur - eebooWORX

Printed in the United States of America
First Edition April 2022

Acknowledgments and Notes

Many thanks to Lee for believing in CINCO DE DIE-O, my first attempt at expanding romance to include mystery - and for welcoming me so warmly into the Desert Palm Press family. It's been great to gather via zoom with sister authors across the states and around the globe, and I can't wait to meet some of my siblings in person at the Left Coast Literary Conference (LCLC) in October. The ongoing efforts to bring us together as a team are much appreciated.

Gracías también to Amaris Cruz who was the first to volunteer to read these pages. She offered some wonderful advice in the form of some helpful suggestions that I took to heart, even if at first her brutal honesty did sting a little –lol!

And to Mich for crafting the cover exactly as I had imagined it and having her creative way with it.

Thanks also to my editor, C.K. King, who I suspect found herself in need of some calming inebriation after enduring my continued difficulty with POV (but I'm in everyone's head as the writer of all the characters, so what's the problem?) and insistent persistence of name-music-movie-and-brand dropping. I like to think of it as *my style*, along with the many uber-long sentences I'm finally learning to make shorter and choppier. At least, I think.

Of course, I must also express gratitude to my wife, Cyndi, who *most always* overlooks all that I don't do when I'm writing.

Last–but not least, some final words for whomever is reading this–I hope you enjoy the coziness of this little San Antonio River Walk mystery buoyed up by the banter of Bobbi and Paige. I quickly came to LOVE these two women (characters) and look forward to sharing more of their adventures with you. They're bound to become embroiled in many entertaining escapades in the future. Thanks for giving them and me a chance.

Happy reading!

Toni

Dedication

For Judy,
who said she'd buy this book for the title alone ;)
May thousands of other would-be readers feel the same way.

Chapter One

"¡AAAAAA – JA – JA – JA - JAI - Y!"

That cathartic, joyous, mariachi *grito* of emotion crowned the accompaniment of trumpets, guitars, violins, and *vihuela*. Thalía's signature song, *Amor a la Mexicana*, appeared to be just what the crowd needed to get everyone out of their seat and on their feet.

I walked to the door and looked out across the water, well, as far as I could see. I'd been busy in the kitchen prepping for the evening's festivities and had missed out on much, so it seemed. In my absence, the boats had been transformed into *trajineras*, much like the colorful, gondolaesque flat bottoms that navigate the Xochimilco canals on the outskirts of Mexico City. Bearing bright decorations in the form of flowers and painted signs, these floating vessels were overflowing with people dancing and singing.

As one after another floated by, beneath showers of serpentine streamers and confetti, I occasionally caught glimpses of the riverbank walkway on the other side. Solitary white candles, deeply ensconced in sanded luminaria bags, lined San Antonio's River Walk. The flickering wicks on the ground and overhead fairy strings provided the perfect lighting for a lovely late afternoon that was slowly giving way to the promise of a festive evening.

I smiled and resigned myself to the fact that it was gonna be a long night, a long weekend for that matter, but fun. April's Fiesta days were always over the top, the perfect prelude to Cinco de Mayo celebrations in downtown San Antonio. The street food, cold Coronas and margaritas, *cumbia* dancing, and all types of Latin American music enticed the throngs. Once it got started, it was impossible to stop. The way drinks were flowing, we barkeeps were bound to make a killing.

Little did I know, with my innocent, idiomatic foreshadow, before the night was over, that prophecy would be fulfilled. The actions of some unknown entity, for some unfathomable reason, would lead me to embark on some amateur sleuthing a la Miss Marple.

I'd just finished salting the rims of another batch of glasses and wiping my hands on the towel thrown casually across my shoulder. One of San Antonio PD's finest strutted through the door. Tall and dark.

Cute, too. I hadn't seen her before. I might enjoy a little afternoon small talk with a stranger.

"*Bienvenida a Beta's*," I welcomed her with more than my usual cheery charm, across a bartop otherwise devoid of human life.

She smiled at me in a friendly manner. Perhaps she'd momentarily forgotten that she was duty-bound to appear stoic and nonplussed by flirtatious behavior. Or, maybe she just didn't recognize it as such. *Have I lost my touch?*

"What brings you here, Officer? Business or pleasure?" I expressed my curiosity, because the park police normally patrolled the river on foot, bike, and boat, not the city police. She failed to answer, so I posed another question, "What can I get you to drink?"

She smiled again. She shouted over the deafening din drifting into my little cantina, "You know, right about now, I wish I could have what I want, to drink that is." *Is she flirting, too?* I wondered at the possible double entendre. "Unfortunately, I'm on duty, hence my blues. I just stopped in to cool off a bit. I hope you don't mind if I sit for a minute or two?"

I looked at her then, I mean really looked at her. Unlike Keith Urban's croon, blue was her color. She looked damn good in it. The hue of her uniform accented the hazel hint in her chestnut-tinted, almond-shaped eyes. I could almost imagine the feel of a tight clump of that audaciously auburn hair all tangled up in a fist of mine. Naturally curly or flat-ironed straight, didn't matter, my fantasies didn't discriminate. I cleared my throat in an attempt to tamp down my lascivious want. Who knew a cop costume could be so form-fitting? And in all the right places?

Finally, my eyes made their way back to her face. Yep, she knew I'd been checking her out. I gave her a little wink. Why not? "Stay as long as you like. If you can't right now, come back soon, when you're on your own time. Whatever you desire will be on me, on *la casa. Mi casa es su casa.*" I opened my arms wide with the invitation, before catching a glimpse of myself in the Beers of Mexico mirror at the end of the bar. She was way out of my league.

As if reading my mind and understanding my bravado was but a cloak to cover those deep-rooted insecurities of mine, she shared her first brilliant deduction, "I take it you must be Beta?"

I slid a condensation-dripping glass filled with ice cold water her way. "That's me, alright. Beta. It's short for Roberta, but my friends all call me Bobbi."

"Thanks for wetting my whistle, Bobbi." She winked again with that salacious smile, before lifting her glass in my direction and draining the hydrating refreshment in a single series of seductive swallows. I became mesmerized by the movement of the water as it quenched its way wantonly down her slender throat. "I just might take you up on that offer. Unfortunately, it'll have to be another day. For now, I'd better get back out there."

As she turned to exit my open door, I followed close behind. I wondered why she'd steered away from my initial inquiry as to her presence on the subterranean level of these mean SA streets. As a proprietor, the happenings were at least some of my business.

The early evening was already sultry and steamy, and that little encounter had left me swooning and sweaty. I was hot and bothered, pitiful in a puddle of pooling drool on *Fantasy Island*. I frantically fanned a fistful (there was that image again) of laminated menus in front of my flustered face and began readying Beta's for the rowdies that were soon to visit me and my little tacos-and-tequila *taberna.* Or, so I hoped.

Thankfully, it wasn't long before my special-occasion regulars drifted in. In no time, their laughter and "gay-ety" pulled me out of the depths of my overactive imagination and into the good-time present of the reality surrounding me.

"Hey Bobbi. How's it goin'? Have you had a chance to get out there yet?" Joseph motioned toward the river. "You want me to watch things for a few, so you can go have a little fun?"

"Thank you, but I'd rather be here with you. You guys are much more entertaining than any rowdy revelers and tipsy tourists could ever be."

"Ain't that the truth," he exclaimed proudly and loudly, as he pulled me into a giant bear hug and gave me a scratchy, whisker-burn kiss on the cheek.

"Margaritas all the way around?"

His answer came in the form of the black American Express he slid across the wood. "You got it babe. You make the best 'ritas on the walk, and you know it." His wink blew away billowy wisps of the last remaining gray clouds that had threatened to rain on my parade and cleared my soul with the force of a little F1 Texas tornado.

"They're on me tonight, so start a tab for us. And keep 'em coming. The night is young, and so are we." He blew another smiling kiss my way, before rejoining his friends at the back table. I poured as fast as I could. The limes I cut juicily slapped on their lips, of the glasses that is, and quickly fell into the bottoms of rapidly emptying barware. Joseph's credit card balance went up and up and up. Cha-ching!

I loved my job, my life. Sure, the occasional out o' towner sometimes stumbled in and maybe made a remark or two about the rundown condition of my place. About me? *There comes that doubt again.* The tourists' unkind, bordering on cruel, comments hurt a little, and from time to time caused me to reconsider my cantina's warm, albeit worn, condition. But this was my home away from home. The place where I'd spent more time than any other was fine by my standards. Maybe that was the problem? Or was it me? I shook it off and headed for the pass.

"Fire up the grill, Marcos. Here comes your first order." I called through the window to my cook in the back. Although no one had requested food yet, with so much alcohol flowing, I insisted they put something in their stomachs. This was a business, my business, and my customers needed a little substance to absorb the liquored nourishment they were currently throwing back and down. *As long as they don't throw it up, it's all good.* Not insisting they eat would make me derelict in my duties and, later, regret missing out on my best chance for any upselling.

When I turned back around, I saw the Back Table Boys signal they were ready for another round. This time, frozen daisies. As I dodged several newcomers on my way to deliver their drinks, I noticed a few more familiar faces had snuck in and joined the crowd.

"Hey Danny. Paul. Hi Robbie. Dean. It's so good to see you guys." I carefully balanced the tray I was carrying in one hand and lightly touched their shoulders and backs as I passed. "I'll be right with you. Thanks for stopping in."

"Oh, Bobbi, what would a Cinco de Mayo celebration be without you? It sure wouldn't be any fun." Danny stood to let a trio of scantily clad women squeeze by. They were obviously wanting action they wouldn't be getting from him or any of the other guys at his table. I noticed the last one seemed to linger as her body s-l-o-w-l-y brushed his backside. If only she knew, her interest and energy were so wasted. The only sensation her home-o-boy felt was irritation at how long it was taking her to shimmy by, evident as he rolled his eyes and waited impatiently to settle in his seat.

I laughed and was thankful to see my two nieces, Guillermina (Billie) and Bety, had arrived to help me out. An *abuelita* with an addiction to *Petticoat Junction* was responsible for their names and mine. I quickly hugged them and pointed to their aprons, before resuming my banter with Danny and the debutantes.

"Here you go, fellas." I placed a big basket of chips in the center of the table along with three generously filled bowls: one with *queso caliente*, another with salsa *picante*, and of course, one with fresh guac', straight outta the avocado.

"Are you trying to fatten us up, woman?" Paul laughed. "You know our kinda crowd likes their men lean and trim."

I chuckled, knowingly. "Don't worry. I'm sure you'll shake it off later. For now, you need to eat something. Otherwise, you might make some foolish mistakes this evening." I laughed loudly before returning to the bar.

From my vantage point there, I surveyed my queendom. While there were plenty of nights I'd witnessed lone strangers attempt to drown their sorrows at my bar, tonight there was no crying, save for the a*ye-yai-yai-ng* of the mariachis. There were no tears in beers, only frosty mugs raised in cheers. I loved seeing and hearing my patrons have such a raucously good time. By the looks of it, even my hardworking *sobrinas* seemed to be enjoying themselves.

* * *

When the sun set and the sky began to darken, I flipped the switch that turned on the little, red-chili-pepper lights I had strung around the ceiling's perimeter and through the door to the patio outside. They gave a warm glow to the festive linens that adorned my tabletops. Striped runners represented every beautiful color of the rainbow. Vibrant hues screamed *mírame a fuerza* in any and every language and to every race, ethnicity, and sexual orientation. "*¡Viva la familia!*" I shouted aloud to both the crowd in general and no one in particular.

Suddenly, a burst of accordion music pulled my attention the way of the musicians. There were always mariachis on the river, but tonight, their trumpets and violins were being blasted away by the Tejano bands that had set up on stages just for the occasion. This was their celebration, a Tex-Mex mix of sound set apart and distinguished by a distinct beat and instruments with more buttons than brass. Was that el Grupo Siggno's "#Hashtag" I heard? If that wasn't Jesse and his rockteño band, whoever was covering was doing a hell of a job.

I swung my hips to the beat, as I moved across the floor. It was getting late, and the hordes of happy revelers were thinning out. They'd move on to places like Cattlemen's and the Thirsty Horse, watering holes that catered to the late-late-night crowds.

"Billie and Bety, thanks for your help. I appreciate it more than you could know." I handed over the money they'd earned from their cash out. "I don't know what I'd do without you girls."

"Same time tomorrow, *Tía*?" They inquired in unison.

"If you're up for it. I expect we'll have crowds nightly all through the weekend."

"*Bueno*, see you then. Bye." The two skipped out, in a race, no doubt, to whatever excitement awaited the much, much, younger-than-me crowd.

I closed up behind them and decided to go out into the night for a while and surround myself with the ongoing celebration. I spent so much time working in my bar that I often forgot how vibrant a big city's nightlife could be. Although currently cluttered with ambulatory vendors and bodies milling about, I could still make out the splendor of architecture that was a fusion of Spanish, Mexican, French, and Modern influences. Downtown San Antonio is a beautiful metropolis. As I neared Market Square, I saw the colorful fabric of some folkloric dancers spin, twirl, and swirl about to the music of strolling musicians. Everywhere I looked, I saw mini piñatas, sombreros, and colorful paper flowers.

Earlier in the day, I'd heard there had been a spicy taco-eating competition going on: tortillas stuffed with green chile chicken *verde*, some combination of serrano slathered in a yellow shishito-lime sauce, and a red-habanero burn through the lining of both your stomach and mouth challenge. The traffic-light colors from green to yellow to red, signaled an increase in heat from go to you-might-want-to-stop. I looked at what was left as a reminder of what had taken place at the booth. Disposable vinyl gloves, goggles, and printed cautions *DO NOT touch your eyes or face* were all part of the culinary contest to determine the winning Heat Master. Jeez, the things people would do. Why torture yourself with food that hot? I wondered what they got out of it—maybe a few seconds on an edited, local television spot?

I looked at one of the signs with the rules and regulations of the contest. *My God! Entrants even had to sign a waiver.* Apparently, the challengers had three minutes to eat the three different tacos. Once they'd finished the last one, they had to wait five minutes (for Cinco de Mayo) before they could dig into bowls of cooling and soothing vanilla ice cream that was scooped as needed. *Talk about southing your mouth.*

No thanks. I prefer taste over temperature. When food is that spicy, your taste buds will be scorched, and you'll taste absolutely *nada*. I shook my head and walked on. Ah, the smells emanating from Juancho's interior, they were more my style. I salivated, as plates of Hatch green chile picadillo and roasted-tomato shredded chicken wafted by, with chasers of blue-corn tortillas in toweled baskets to keep them warm.

By the looks of it, some of these people had most likely been partying all day long. I passed by a young woman who stood at the top of some concrete stairs. Likely a good idea, since the too-drunks stumbling at the foot of them probably wouldn't be able to manage such a reach. Nearby, other singles and couples twirled and swayed. Some moved with their arms free and others encircling the waists of nonexistent lovers or each other, while dancing around a San Antonio River Walk regular dressed like Elvis. I'm not sure how that king fit in the picture. In my opinion, the man might have better repped as Emiliano Zapata or some other much revered Mexican for the occasion, but whatever. I noticed all the men had either a can or a bottle in hand, continuing to get their *borracho* on.

"*Suavecito, suavecito,*" the young woman sang Laura León's classic, cumbia tropical from the '80s. *What the heck. I might as well date myself by knowing that one*. I walked on, surrounded by a surplus of Spurs jerseys and caps. I don't recall ever having seen so much headgear. I headed for the next bottleneck of people stalled at a table where one of the restaurant chefs was mixing what he called a kiwi-lemon cooler made with Herradura Silver. He mixed the agave-sweet tequila with muddled fruits, ice, and a splash of Topo Chico. I passed by Café Olé's sixty-ounce, EFFEN Cucumber margarita, which boasted thirteen shots each of tequila and vodka, with your choice of thirty-seven types to choose from. Cinco de Mayo had definitely given way to Drinko de Mayo. I figured it was time for me to head home before these drunkards hit the asphalt on the same roads on which I'd be driving.

Leaving the Thirsty Aztec in my rearview mirror, I looked ahead to the majestic Aztec Theatre, now visible via the cracked windshield of my truck. An uninformed tourist, maybe even many San Antonians, might never know the grandeur that lies hidden within the nondescript exterior at the corner of Commerce and St. Mary's. The interior of the Mayan revival theater houses a myriad of replicas and images: a maize goddess, Zapotec inspired sculpture, and a gilded carving of

Quetzalcoatl, among many others. The historic auditorium offers an explosion of Mesoamerican culture.

My navigation of the one-ways took me past San Fernando Cathedral, a beautiful place of worship, but a little lacking in heartfelt teachings. I felt a moment of sadness that the church denies an unconditional welcome for Dignity and the LGBTQ+ community, that, in this day and age of awareness and enlightenment, so many could be blinded to love's reality. I wondered what it would take to convince them that love is love, that we are all children of the same God, brothers and sisters of the same human race.

Chapter Two

BOBBI HAD BEEN HOME for hours by the time verbs and nouns began buzzing through The Sentinel's newsroom like bolts of electricity. The people and press were humming and hopping for a Thursday night, but then it was Cinco de Mayo, or at least had been a few hours earlier in the day. What the editorial staff knew that the still-partying people didn't, was that the happy, holiday-fun photographs so carefully situated for prominent display on the front page were being slushed out, dumped and bumped by a much darker and more sinister headline.

Veteran reporter, Kevin Jameson, was all over the story. He pounded away at the keyboard with unbridled fury, all too well aware that the clock was ticking. Unlike many on deadline in the newsroom, he found himself inspired by music. Linkin Park's "Numb" nearly rattled the window next to his small cubicle as he typed, his fingers flying far faster than the song's beat.

At more than six feet tall, the sandy-haired, freckle-faced boy next door had found his niche at the newspaper, straight out of college. High school coaches had clamored for him to play basketball from his freshmen to his senior years. While good on the court, sports were never his thing. He'd always preferred the satisfaction of being able to sink a perfect sentence, one that created a visual *swoosh* better than any three-point buzzer beater. He happily hung up his hoops jersey and majored in journalism. He knew, early on, he wanted to be a writer. That someday had been a decade in the making.

While his parents were dismayed that he didn't take the athletics scholarships and considered his unprofessional choices irresponsible, he didn't let them dash his hopes or change his plans. He had been a disappointment to them for most of his life, falling in with the wrong teen crowds, then choosing solitary isolation, nothing had pleased them about his life. He'd show them. This breaking news story would be the base for his multitiered cake. Its filling would be an exposé that was bound to lead him to journalistic glory. He wouldn't stop until he iced that cake and made the front page himself, photographed holding his Pulitzer Prize. That was his dream and had been from his first story-writing days.

"You got that piece ready yet, Jameson?" The editor was nervously pacing the floor, breathing down Kevin's neck as the young man frantically typed.

"Almost, sir. I just need a few more minutes."

"That's good because that's about all you've got."

By way of police reports and other news that had come in from those who'd been at the scene of the crime, and with a phenomenal photograph to run alongside his paragraphs, he'd cobbled together the best breaking news story he'd ever written. Thank God, he'd been in the right place at the right time. He put a period at the end of the last sentence and sent the story on its way. The adrenaline leaked from his body and tiredness hit him like a ton of bricks. For tonight, his job was done. If he were lucky, maybe he could squeeze in a few hours of shut-eye before the arrival of another day in which he'd triumph to do it all over again.

***

While most bar owners and workers lived the life of vampires, I was the exception to that rule. I always rose by the sun's dawning light, no matter what time I'd gone to bed. Thus, I was one of the first to see the news splashed across the top of The Sentinel's morning edition. After retrieving the newspaper from its landing place outside my cantina's door, I unbagged and unrolled the purveyor of print journalism, before setting it aside while I completed my rituals. As I poured coffee grounds into a filter, the first thing I noticed was the size of the headline's print. Before I'd even read the words, I knew this news had to be big. Finally, when I had my first cup poured and could give the article my full and undivided attention, I was shocked to read

Cinco de Mayo turns Cinco de Die-O

WTF...What kind of newspaper is this? I wanted to get the gist of the story before my friends came crashing my pre-brunch party. I love them, but they are nothing short of a bunch of *metiche* merchants. I quickly read the article, which did have a slightly less sensational and smaller subtitle beneath the one that spanned the top of the newspaper's front page.

Body Found Floating in the San Antonio River

Authorities are working to determine what led to the death of an unidentified man found floating in the San Antonio River, near downtown, early Friday morning. Determination of a cause and manner of death is pending. According to police reports, the body was found shortly after 2 a.m. by a group of people exiting a popular bar in the vicinity. According to San Antonio Police spokesperson, Sgt. Caleb McAllister, the approximately thirty-year-old man was wearing a tank top and shorts and had no shoes on his feet. No obvious signs of trauma were found on the body.

For having such big words hovering over it, the story itself was short and lacking in content. *Oh well, I guess the picture is worth a thousand words.* I studied the photo intently and, forsaking all but the first paragraph, wondered if a drunken reveler had merely fallen in after a night of debauchery. The autopsy had yet to be performed, so who could say? I was still morbidly staring at the grainy image, when my nosy neighbor from the gift shop next door, Diane Maldonado of The Blue Burro, raced over my threshold and nearly collided with my cup of Cafe Olé.

"Oh my God, Bobbi, Did you see—" she stopped when she saw that I had the newspaper spread out before me. but soon after again screeched as she rattled on about the *pobrecito*. Callous as it seems, my first thoughts were not of the corpse amid the calla lilies, but of business, and wondering of what this news would do to it. *Will the merriment be stopped?* It was far closer to 5:00 a.m. than 5:00 p.m., but I sure could use a drink of a different nature, comprised of something much stronger than the caffeine in coffee.

"I just put on a pot of jitter juice. Would you like to join me in a cup, Di?"

Maybe for the time being I should call her by her full first name.

"What? Huh? Sure." She answered, as she studied the photograph that accompanied the news story. "That'd be delightful, Bobbi. So, you're the sleuth among us, what do you think happened?"

I paused for a moment, wondering how many of my thoughts, fears, and concerns I should divulge. After all, while I considered Diane a friend in the business sense, even with an endowment I'd often admired, we weren't exactly what you'd call bosom buddies.

"Maybe it was just some old borracho who'd had too much to drink, too much of a good time."

"Yeah, maybe you're right. Poor guy, I hope that's all."

By the time noon neared, the other member of my almost-daily lunch bunch had made an appearance and was sharing his thoughts and expressing his shock over the discovery. With his jaw nearly dropped to the table, I barely managed to squeeze a plate under it.

"Careful," I cautioned, "it's hot."

I hoped they wouldn't Google shrimp *alambre* tacos and discover they weren't a Beta's original recipe. "Buen provecho compadres. Let me know what you think. This is today's and tonight's specialty. And, if all doesn't go so well, it might also be around for tomorrow's lunch, and maybe even dinner. We'll see."

"Oh, Bobbi, please." Charlie Owens, the owner of Rainbow Reads, rolled his eyes before sinking his teeth and tastebuds into the contents of the tortilla, straight offa the *comal*. His eyes rolled upward as if he were searching for the secret ingredients in his brows. "Exquisite. This time, *mujer*, you have truly outdone yourself."

Diane opened the taco to peek inside and there found shrimp, of course, but also bits of bacon, chorizo, and cheese. "¿Oaxaca?" She fished for the type, as she daintily bit into my culinary concoction and devilishly stretched the white cheese wires from the Talavera plate to her mouth. A response from me that would reveal my secret ingredient was not forthcoming.

"Whatever it is, it's delicious. You're sure to run out before the night is done."

I beamed with pride and joy, hoping my customers would agree. That is, if they found themselves lured away from those better known and advertised Market Square restaurants long enough to find Beta's.

Our conversation, like the melted cheese, was pulled around a myriad of hot topics from the previous night's financial successes to the morning's news about the untimely drowning.

"Have you heard if the body's been identified yet?"

"Not yet, and from what I read there was nothing on him to help investigators out, nor has anyone filed a missing-persons report. Of course, he was an adult."

"I hate to sound cold-hearted, ladies," Charlie chimed in, "but, I doubt our clientele will let this dampen their spirits. Especially since, so far, it appears to be an accidental death by drowning. So, I say cheers to another prosperous evening. Bottoms up!"

Soon, the conversation ran its course and the gastronomic gang filtered out. I reached for the newspaper and snapped it back open. I had just finished rereading the first paragraph in its entirety, when the sun's light, which I was using as a lamp in the cavernous darkness of my that's-how-I-keep-it-cool establishment, was suddenly blocked.

I looked over the readers perched on the tip of my nose and swallowed nervously, hoping my cotton mouth would be able to speak to the object that had created a total eclipse of my heart and now stood in my doorway. "Greetings Officer. You know, if we're gonna keep meeting like this, a non-ranked more personal name by which I can call you would be most helpful and much appreciated."

"Hello, Bobbi. My apologies. I guess I didn't realize I hadn't introduced myself when we first met." She extended what turned out to be a surprisingly soft, smooth, and well-manicured hand. I tenderly took said hand and maybe, just maybe, held on to it a little longer than I should have. I'm not sure what I had expected, perhaps the roughness and toughness I thought would be part and parcel of an enforcer of the law. Maybe she lotioned and wore gloves. The velvety tones of her voice matched the satiny suppleness I was feeling.

"It's Paige, I'm Paige."

At that precise moment, my attention was diverted to the name badge she wore pinned over the pocket of her ample breast. I looked at her face. "No way," I blurted out a little louder than I had intended, no doubt a result of the disbelief at the surname I found there.

"Yes. I'm afraid so. Paige Turner." She chuckled at what had to have been a recurrent revelatory explanation. "What can I say? My mother is a librarian and consummate bibliophile, who was apparently shameless when it came to naming her baby."

I whispered internally, at least I hoped I wasn't heard, my offer to gladly share my name with her. Although, I admitted that it'd be best if we first got to know each other a little better. My eyes danced across some finely formed hips as some truth-telling words of Shakira came to mind. I could envision us trying out those shiny handcuffs.

While I may not have spoken my thoughts aloud, I wondered if she'd heard them. My eyes had fallen and fixated on the pair of silver bracelets she carried at her belt. *Who needs Fifty Shades of Gray*? From where I stood, shackled by a middle-aged state of hyperventilation and overactive imagination, *Fifty Minutes with Paige* was sure to be a far better read.

Thankfully, her voice shook me out of my mental reverie.

"Anyway, Bobbi, while admittedly it's indeed a pleasure to be here, business is the reason I've come."

She nodded at the open newspaper.

"*¡No me diga!* You're on the case of the drowned man?" The reminder of the tragic event served to douse the flames burning ardently inside me.

"As a matter of fact, yes. I'm here to see if anything or anyone from last night may have left an impression on you. Do you remember seeing anything unusual or different?"

"Only you." I responded all too quickly and without thinking.

"I'm sorry," she replied, just as I was hoping she hadn't heard, "am I honestly so unusual or different?"

"No. No. Well, yes. But, in a good way." Oh hell, there was no graceful way out of this mess I'd made of words. I couldn't very well tell her, *you were the only one who's occupied my every waking and sleeping thought since you first walked through that door.* No, that would only make matters worse. The twinkling, mischievous glint in her eyes kinda made me think she already knew what I was thinking.

"Well, if you happen to remember anything, please let me know. We have no idea who the man was or what might have happened to him. Meanwhile, I'm going to make my rounds here and see if I can jiggle anything loose"—She paused dramatically there and moved to shake away the long, lovely locks that had fallen, ever so slightly, in front of her beautiful, green brown eyes. The disturbance caused a tsunami-like, eye-engaging movement. "In the minds of your neighboring business owners and operators."

Okay. There was no doubt in my mind that Officer Paige Turner was, indeed, messing with me. She could have chosen so many other words, but no, she had to paint *that* picture, leave me with *that* image. The one I wouldn't soon forget and would likely never erase completely from my apparently dirty mind. *Qué sinvergüenza soy.*

I reached for the CD player and bowed to the king of cumbia, Fito Olivares. As "La Sabrosona" played, I acknowledged to the world that there was definitely a conspiracy theory to explain what was happening to me and my life.

If you don't believe me, look up the meaning of the song's title.

And all was well, until the next day when the next body was found.

Chapter Three

WOMAN'S BODY FOUND AT LA VILLITA'S ARNESON RIVER THEATRE

"OKAY, THIS IS LOOKING less like an accident now. Let's look at what we've got," I greeted our group of amateur crime solvers as we were coming to be known, at least by me. Charlie and Di were the other members of my puny posse. We put our heads together over bowls of menudo (some say for the *crudo*) as we looked at the reported facts and attempted to puzzle out the mystery.

Jane Doe was found rolled up in a tortilla blanket (yes, they do exist), and tucked neatly behind a row of potted red flowers (bougainvillea?) that curved along the Arneson River Theatre's stone stage. A tourist out early to take pictures had wondered what the unsightly tannish blur was that kept appearing in her otherwise well-framed shots. She went for a closer look. Poor woman. What a souvenir of the city.

I found myself wondering if someone was trying to make a statement or send us midriver merchants a message. After all, the bodies seemed to be confined to an area that surrounded us. But why? And, if so, what? And, wasn't there a better way to do it than Al Pacino style? I didn't relished the thought of finding a horse's head in my bed. Although, at this point, my bed could use a little of any kind of action. It had been a while.

Meanwhile, back in the kitchen, Carola, my part-time cook, was toasting and roasting tear-and-cough producing chiles verdes on the comal. The smoke was starting to make us choke, but not yet enough to run us out.

"Why here? Why now?" Diane dabbed at her watering eyes and covered her running nose and mouth. "Do you think the timing is a coincidence? Or could there be a connection to the date, the occasion? What do we know about Cinco de Mayo?"

Charlie rambled, reading from the small screen of his cell phone. "Well, historically speaking, and I quote a liberally adlibbed Wikipedia here, the fifth of May, at least in the land of our neighbor to the south, and I don't mean Presa Street, commemorates Mexico's unlikely victory over French forces at the Battle of Puebla on May 5, 1862. By the looks of it, it's not celebrated much at all, even in Puebla, these days. Here in San Antonio and all the other cities with large Latino populations in the States, it's become a day to honor Mexican culture and pride."

"Ha!" I couldn't keep that hearty exclamation from forcing itself out of my mouth. "Who do they think they're kidding?" I tossed my two pesos in. "It's an excuse to drink in excess, party hard, and have a good time. Maybe engage in a little hokey pokey or hanky panky, whatever floats your boaty or booty. That's what it's all about. Not that I'm complaining."

An unexpected breeze chose that precise moment to blow through the door, flapping the plastic banners I'd hung overhead. Only in one's wildest imagination did they even remotely resemble authentic *papel picado*. I hoped that chill air wasn't the long expired spiritual breaths of any angry soldiers my flippant remarks may have offended.

"By the way, has anyone seen Sam?" I asked.

Samuel Delgado was the restaurateur of my nemesis, La China Poblana. By nature of physical proximity, he was one of us. By all other measures, he wasn't, in any way. He had no qualms letting that be known to anyone and everyone. He thought his restaurant better than our low-life establishments. No doubt, he was out trying to have the yellow, crime-scene tape removed from in front of his fine dining establishment, much like he'd managed to do with the scavenging river ducks. Not that his place offered any outdoor seating. No, in his once-spoken words, "It's far too refined and elegant for such a plebeian pastime as feeding the waterfowl."

"Come to think of it, I haven't seen him for a few days. I got so busy with my own preparations. I had no idea what was going on with anyone else. Do you think we should check in on him?"

"Be my guest, Diane." I invited. "Or, well, his. And, please, give him my regards."

"Tsk, Bobbi baby, when are the two of you ever going to play nice together?" Charlie wondered aloud.

"Well, let's see. According to the calendar, it's now siete de Mayo, so check back on the twelfth of never. Maybe by then, we'll be sporting our BFF bracelets, but don't bet on it."

The gang chuckled, carried their empty bowls to the kitchen, and once again profusely thanked me for their sated stomachs. It was time for all of us to get to work and open our doors wide to the patrons we could only hope we would soon welcome inside. "Let's get the party started," I announced to everyone within earshot. By the looks of it, as I scanned my eatery's interior, that was exactly no one.

Seeking solace, I found Pink's subliminally inspiring dance track, popped into my beat-up old CD player, and prepared to get my own private fiesta on. If that's what had to be, so be it. The sorry Sony that had seen better days and borne melodic witness to its share of wicked weekend nights now claimed space on the highest shelf behind my bar, above the many glass bottles there. It may not be the most technologically advanced or digitally enhanced of musical machines, but it still did the job.

The song had no sooner stopped, than my thoughts pounded and pulsated. I rewound the images in my memory of the last few nights and looked at them carefully, each and every one. After Danny and the guys had left on Thursday, there were a number of unknowns who had come in and out of my bar. Most were on the younger side, the typical party crowd simply out to have a good time. There was, however, one older gentleman who stood out in my memories, mostly for his out of place attire. The three piece he'd been wearing didn't register as being odd at the time. I often serve businessmen and women in suits, when they escape stuffy conferences taking place in the hotels nearby. *That's usually only at lunch time.* The evenings were almost always exclusively casual: shorts, t-shirts, and tank tops, especially during these months. Late afternoons until well past midnights were so unbearably humid and hot. Not only that, but he was alone. I hoped to remember to mention him to the others and see if any of them had seen him, too.

My meandering through the memories of my mind stalled, as customers appeared and demanded my attention. Soon, I forgot about the mystery man altogether. He disappeared from my mind without a trace.

By the time the afternoon rush had disappeared, many in search of a vacant seat on a riverboat tour, I finally got the chance to sit and open the three days' or more worth of mail stacked beside the register and almost completely forgotten. As I sifted through the envelopes and sorted the bills I wouldn't yet be paying, the words of one of the megaphoned men outside caught my ears. Once again, I pushed the pile aside.

"You may recognize this as Selena's Bridge. Not Gomez but Quintanilla-Pérez, South Texas's much-loved queen of Tejano music.

The bridge had a bit role in the movie in which J. Lo played the Latina star."

As always happened when I heard her name mentioned, the needle in my old-school mind dropped in the groove of "I Could Fall in Love." I sat swaying and swooning to a mental replay of that sweet icon's crooning. Of course, as fate and fantasy would have it, who should walk in...

"Don't tell me. Let me guess. You're here to taco 'bout the latest body."

The dressed-down police officer looked at me with more than a little disappointment in her alluring, albeit somewhat sadly expressive, eyes.

"I'm sorry, I don't mean to make light of the matter. It's just how I cope with near-death experiences. And they are getting a little too close for comfort these days."

Dressed in a top-three-buttons-open button down, some sequined jeans, and wait—Were they Tecovas?—Turner was looking mighty fine out of uniform. A cowgirl, be still my now thudding heart. She was apparently comfortable in her casual street wear, I deduced, as she pulled out a chair uninvited. Making herself at home, she sat seductively by my side.

As good as she looked, I could tell the upwardly mobile river walk body count was bringing her down. She sighed heavily. "I'm afraid I can't tell you any more than what's already been made public, mostly because that's all we know. I stopped by hoping you might have thought of something."

Oh, if she only knew how I'd love to be her cohort in crime solving.

I told her about the mysterious man but hadn't yet had a chance to see if the others had any more information. All I had for her was a lead to nowhere, and she already had more than enough of those, so ... Sensing she was about to get up and go, I got up to get her a lemonade, hoping she'd stay a while and savor my sweet offering. "This is the best non-alcoholic drink I have," I told her before my traitorous eyes betrayed any innocence I'd retained from a long abandoned youth. They drifted down her shirt front, stopping only where her cleavage started. "I squeezed the lemons fresh myself this morning."

Turner smiled, appearing to enjoy the attention, so I felt her up. I mean, out! I felt her out regarding our unfortunate, current situation. "I and my fellow business operators, here on the river, have been trying to find any connections that might tie the two bodies together. We're racking our brains in search of a reason why this might be happening here, especially now." She looked at me with such hopeful eyes, I hated to tell her that so far we had come up empty handed. Speaking of hope, I sure hope God will forgive me for what next came out of my mouth.

"You know, there *is* someone you might want to take a closer look at." I described Sam's suspicious disappearance. "He used to come around to hang and chat with the rest of us, and none of us have seen him lately."

She pulled the smallest little spiral pad I'd ever seen out of her pocket and clicked her pen into action, ready and waiting for me to throw the man under the zigzagging VIA bus I was haphazardly driving. "Samuel Delgado," I told her and watched as she wrote his name. "He owns La China Poblana, the restaurant across the river." I pointed to where the hostess stood at the outdoor greeting station. From the red, white, and green ribbons wrapped around her waist length braids to the matching, sequined dress that twirled each time she sashayed away, the hostess resembled the restaurant's namesake. I shook my head. "I don't know how the hell she wears that thing in this heat. That getup on me would have got up and gone by now."

Turner smiled, appearing amused by my seemingly endless litany of entertaining, idiomatic expressions. La China Poblana wouldn't open for dinner until five o'clock. I wondered if Turner would hang out with me until then. Unfortunately, she screeched her chair back and stood.

"Thank you for the refreshing drink and for always being so welcoming. Please, let me know if you think of anything else." She closed her notebook and tapped it against the palm of her other hand before putting it away. "You never know what information might turn out to be more than it appears."

I swear, her eyes sparkled as she smiled at me before leaving.

I can only wonder …. Damn it, Selena! Not now.

Chapter Four

HE FOLDED THE NEWSPAPER in half, then again, after reading the lead story on the front page. With gleaming eyes, he thrust his jaw forward and held his head high. Satisfied with the job he'd done, his thoughts turned immediately to the one that awaited doing. He enjoyed challenging himself, always doing more than was expected of him, sometimes even more than was wanted. Now, how could he outdo what he had already done? He opened the paper and found his answer on an inside page.

***

Kevin Jameson's father, David, greeted his first born. "Well, well, well, if it isn't the prodigal son," as the reporter crossed the threshold into the bungalow that had been his childhood home. He had never felt welcomed there, even during his boyhood days.

"The problem with that comparison, Dad, is that I'm not sorry for what I've done."

"And to what might you be referring this time, Clark Kent?"

"You'll find out soon enough."

"Now, now," Celeste Jameson interrupted the exchange between her husband and son. "Let's not set that kind of tone for the evening, shall we? Come here, Kevin. I haven't seen you in so long. I'm glad you could make it this evening."

"Happy birthday, Mom." He kissed her on the cheek and pulled a small, wrapped gift from his pocket.

"Kevin, you didn't have to. I know things are tight right now."

"They wouldn't be if he'd listened to us," shouted his father from across the room.

"Come on, dear," his mother intervened, "let's go to the kitchen."

"Smells wonderful, Mom. I don't get much but fast food and microwave meals these days. I've missed your cooking."

"Well, why don't you help me finish setting the table? Dinner is almost ready, and Tommy will be here any minute."

Of course, why hadn't he expected his younger brother would be joining them? That son had listened to his parents and was now at the end of his senior year at Duke, riding free on a full scholarship.

"How long has it been since he's been home?"

She didn't have to think long. "He was here for Christmas, but you weren't. Why not? We missed you over the winter holidays."

"Deadlines, Mom," Kevin gave his usual excuse. "The news never stops."

He wondered how he'd make it through agonizingly stretched-out moments of his father's table talk. Kevin had stopped coming home, long ago, for that reason. It was so obvious who the fair-haired child of the family was, the adored and much-loved, doted-on heir and offspring. Tommy was the one they could always count on, the one who would go far in his chosen field of study. Kevin couldn't even remember what his brother had ultimately decided on as a major, but he knew it was something that would bring in big money. He would be reminded over dinner, soon and sure enough.

Just then, the sound of the back door opening caused them both to look that way. "Hi Mom, Dad. I'm home!" Tommy burst through the door like he always had, larger than life and louder than any of the rest of them. He was always so full of emotional exuberance. So unlike Kevin, but then he had every reason to be. David was instantly out of his chair and pulling Tommy into a big bear hug, while their mother moved in for a customary kiss long before Tommy even noticed Kevin was in the room. Kevin stared at them, silently. He stared through them, beyond the pain and into their joyous space, which he had seldom shared.

"Hey Kev. Long time, man. I can't wait to catch up." Tommy walked across the room and grabbed Kevin by the hand, pulling him into a one-armed man hug. Two pats on his back announced the greeting was over and done.

"Glad you could make it, son." David's genuine welcome for Tommy was intentionally said loud enough for Kevin to hear.

While the men were saying hello to one another, Celeste put the food on the table. "Dinner's ready gentlemen. Take your seats and fill your plates. I made plenty, so dig in. Take and eat all you want."

A spread of comfort food at its finest filled the table. Tender and falling-apart pot roast sat in its own tasty juice, alongside carrots and onions, with some mashed potatoes. The bowls were massive, and for that Kevin's appetite was grateful.

Tommy inhaled his first serving before exclaiming, "This is delicious, Mom."

"I bet you don't get food like this in North Carolina," his father wagered.

"No way. This kinda cooking only comes from Mom's table. God, how I've missed it. And all of you."

His mother laughed. "Don't think I didn't notice we were an afterthought."

From there, David took over the direction of their conversation. "So, tell us about your studies, son, about basketball, about East Coast life, about your plans for the future."

"Well, I've been interning at RTI and am pretty sure I have a secure job offer on the horizon, after graduation. To which, by the way, I hope you're coming?"

"Wouldn't miss it. What are you doing with the company?"

"Web design, and I love it."

"Any other loves?" Celeste wanted to know.

"Well, I have been exclusively dating since New Year's Eve."

"And we're just now hearing about this? Tell us all about her."

They seemed to have forgotten Kevin was there. No one looked his way. No one inquired about his job. He ate and watched in silence, as he was reminded of yet another reason why he'd stopped coming home. None of them thought anything he did was of interest. He doubted they even read the paper or had any idea of his work or accomplishments. Oh well, he didn't need their accolades or praise. He didn't need or want them. All he wanted was to get through this meal and go home.

As the Jameson family gathering entered the apple-pie-dessert phase, dinner was just being served at La China Poblana, where Turner anxiously waited to speak with Samuel Delgado.

***

With no time to waste, Turner approached the banners of red, white, and green at exactly 5:00 p.m. The colors of México's flag adorned the entrance to La China Poblana. The hostess at the outdoor podium stood ready to greet and seat patrons. It appeared Turner would be the first. The legendary Asian fashionista, after whom the restaurant was named and whom Turner had Googled while waiting, had added an eastern flair to Spanish colonial closets. She'd been taken by pirates in the 1600s, then bought by Spaniards, who transported her to the Mexican city of Puebla. Fast forward four centuries, and today's hostess was giving Turner *Ojo.* Turner was not properly attired for a place that served haute cuisine.

Of course, I could see all of this from my little dive bar that served mostly *antojitos* and street tacos. I had to laugh, when Turner pulled her badge out of her back pocket and showed it to the suddenly shrinking sentry. I could almost hear the girl's embarrassment, as her nail-tipped fingers flapped and fluttered with profuse apology before she disappeared into the bowels of the building, likely in search of Delgado himself.

While she waited, Turner lifted one of the weighty, leather menus. I knew they boasted of regional dishes that had put Puebla on the map: various moles, *chiles en nogada, pipían verde*, and for dessert, *tortitas de Santa Clara.* I felt my own self shrinking in culinary comparison and imagined Turner to be won over by the doubtlessly delectable options. The food served there put mine to shame. There were no ifs, ands, or buts about it.

Just as I turned to commiserate with my paltry plates of *pollo asado*, nachos *compuestos* at their best-os, and triflingly trite tacos, I caught a glimpse of the proprietor of La China Poblana. Ever disgustingly debonair, he greeted my *mujer* with the charm of a piranha. His garish, slicked-back, poorly dyed raven hair and pencil-thin mustache were only part of his self-anointed Foodie Overlord persona. Hands up, utensils down. I sighed, knowing there was no comparison between the constellations of his online reviews and those generated by my starless little greasy spoon. *And that, my friends, is how a fool and her honey are soon parted.*

***

"Good afternoon, Mr. Delgado," Turner greeted the restaurant's owner, observing both the man and his behavior, as well as the quickly filling tables that surrounded her.

"*Buenas tardes*, Officer."

After she was sure he'd seen it, Turner put away her shield. For the second time that day, she found herself being scrutinized by disapproving eyes. *It must be a job requirement.*

"*¿En qué puedo servirle?* What can I do for you, while it is still possible for me to personally attend to you? I will soon find myself called away by the demands of my appetent patrons."

Thinking it best to dispence with small talk and make the most of the little time it seemed he'd give her, she addressed the overly gallant, yet simultaneously unsavory, proprietor. "I trust, by now, you've heard about the bodies that have been found here on our city's River Walk."

"Yes, of course. It's all over the news. So far, it hasn't seemed to affect *my* business, but time will tell. Have you found the culprit?"

"As a matter of fact, that's why I'm here."

Delgado knitted his brows into a deep pucker, as he waited to hear the reason for Turner's untimely interruption.

"I've been talking to all the merchants here along this section of the river, hoping to find someone who saw or knows something that can help us out with our investigation."

A gentle smile reached eyes beneath a now-smooth forehead. "Well, I'm afraid I'll be of no use to you then. I've only recently returned from a trip to Mexico, where I went to savor and explore new ingredients and recipes so I can keep my menu fresh. Those who come to dine with me expect only the finest of *comida poblana*."

At his haughty admission, Delgado looked toward the entrance, where the line of people backed out the door and onto the sidewalk. He used that awareness as an excuse to promptly put an end to the discussion.

"I'm terribly sorry, Officer Turner, but I need to attend to my newly arriving guests. You understand, I'm sure."

With no reason to further detain him, Turner nodded. "Of course."

"Please stay and dine with us, or come back at a time that's more convenient and enjoy a meal on me. It would be my pleasure to introduce you to a much more pleasing cuisine than you can find elsewhere on San Antonio's River Walk."

"Yes, well, thank you for the invitation and your time."

***

Delgado walked with her to the door. He clapped one hand on her shoulder and shook hers hand with the other. I knew he could see me, because I saw that snotty and conceited glint in his beady little predator eyes. If there were to be another death, I hoped the victim would be found poisoned by one of his overpriced plates. Even better, Delgado himself could choke on a splinter from the stick permanently stuck up his pompous ass. I immediately made the sign of the cross over my heart and begged forgiveness of *Dios todo poderoso* for my less than Christian thoughts and desires.

Awaiting the lightning bolt I was sure would come from heaven above, I watched Turner walk away to a nearby bench. After looking at her phone's screen, as if searching for some sign of divine intervention, she appeared to swipe an app closed. She was looking around from her bench seat. Out of uniform, she could easily be mistaken for almost any ordinary tourist, unprepared and inappropriately dressed for San Antonio's suffocatingly unbearable, triple-digit temperatures. She seemed to be people watching. Many did on the *río*. It was the perfect place for such a pastime, but how could she possibly know who to look for or what was out of place? Had she been frequenting this area for far longer than I realized?. Hmmm ...

Not wanting to appear like a *chismosa* gathering grains of scandal, I abandoned my admiration station. I hoped my mind would soon be distracted by customers. In an attempt to draw more in, I had requested Billie design an advertisement for the night's specialty, gastronomically irresistible and *estómago*-stretching, hand-patted gorditas. I had highlighted the available varieties: refried beans and cheese, picadillo, carne asada, and shredded chicken. I mused at how the masa, once cooked on the comal, became a lot like me, subtly crispy on the outside while still a little soft within. After placing the color print in the clear case beside my open door, I turned to see shoulder-to-shoulder people strolling the sidewalks of the river.

"Marcos! Stoke the fire back there." Maybe some delicious smells wafting out of this place will draw people in."

"Ay, Ay, seño."

Given his non-gender conforming nor marital status-revealing salute, I realized he didn't know much about me at all. But then, I didn't know much about him either. I suspected he had no idea whether I was single, married, divorced, straight, or gay. Maybe he wasn't sure if I was male or female. Oh well, ours was one of the few relationships in my life that worked. He showed when he was scheduled and did what he was expected to do. I paid him every other Friday, and that was all that mattered.

I looked in the mirror and scrutinized the image I saw there. I wondered how others saw me, when all I could focus on was an unplucked, unshaved upper lip and eyebrows that would soon resemble Frida Kahlo's. In a last-ditch effort to make my womanhood stand out loud and proud, I put my hands under my ample, if downward-bound, breasts. I pulled and pushed them up, up, up. Higher and higher. Eat your heart out Madonna. Of course, without her leather and conical reinforcements, keeping them in that position would prove to be the real challenge.

Thankfully, the trick seemed to work, the trick of captivating olfactory audiences, that is. Either that, or the arrival of starving students sporting rival University of Texas, Texas A&M, and UTSA gear was merely coincidental. Regardless, it was well appreciated. I dropped what I was doing, literally, and got to work.

Chapter Five

BECAUSE HIS WAS A different type of business, Charlie could sit back and relax while on the clock. He did occasionally stand to greet browsers who entered his bookstore, but only if he sensed his well-intentioned attention wouldn't run them off.

Although Rainbow Reads was, in truth, an intentional nod to the LGBTQ+ community, he had amassed a gathering of other loyal patrons, some of whom fell more to the other end of the spectrum. The multicolored arc that served as the entry led to a pot of gold in the form of his large selection of indie prints. A yellow brick road wound 'round the store's interior, carving out spaces that catered to children's books, fantasy, and some carefully selected mainstream, adult fiction.

Expressly for the holiday week, he had created a special display just inside the front door. There, he'd prominently put forward such titles as *Erased Faces* by Graciela Limón and *Sor Juana's Second Dream* by Alicia Gaspar de Alba. Carefully placed light-catching prisms and colorful candles enhanced the display.

That's where he was, straightening, *oh, the irony of the word,* things out, when he noticed a man at the rear of the store. Charlie didn't think he'd ever seen the man in his store, nor anywhere else. The stranger was a relatively tall man. Not wanting to seem intrusive, Charlie only chanced a glance every now and again, until the man vacated the shop. While Charlie hoped he hadn't scared him away, there was something a little unsettling about the lone visitor who'd suddenly and silently appeared. *When did he come in? How long was he lurking about? How did he slip by, while I was watching?* Strange, and interesting. *I'll bring it up tomorrow at Bobbi's breakfast.* He had yet to eat dinner and his stomach gurgled loudly at the reminder.

***

After leaving the bookstore, the man ducked into Diane's shop. He'd never seen so many burros, and wondered *Do people collect them?*

Do they have a significance? Why blue? He stopped and looked closer at one. In a word, he was completely flummoxed.

"*He-llo-o.*" From somewhere in the back of the store a woman's soprano voice sang out. "Is there something I can help you find?" Diane queried the man, who watched her approach and gently returned the ceramic donkey to where he'd found it.

"Oh, no thank you. I'm just looking. Although I must say, I'm intrigued by your shop's inventory."

Diane laughed heartily. "Well, what I call it is what you get, for the most part. Except for the color of my donkeys, as I suspect you've already noticed. I love burros, and blue happens to be my favorite color. Since the animals don't come in that color, naturally, save for Milne's Eeyore, I have to settle for renditions of the natural ones." At that, she took him on a verbal, if stationary, tour of her gift store. "As you can see, I cater to burros of all sizes and materials, in a range of prices." She walked to where he stood and placed her hand on the ass he'd earlier had his hands on. "For some reason, this one seems to get the most attention. But as you can see, I have many others, some of porcelain, others of stone, ceramic, fabric, all imaginable and unfathomable representations of these small but hardy pack animals."

Diane babbled on, "Are you familiar with the works of Lladró?"

"I can't say that I am."

"The lighted case by the register holds the collection I have for sale. Their handmade porcelain is crafted in the Valencia region of Spain." She bid him to follow her so he could see the exquisite pieces more closely and truly appreciate the quality of their craftsmanship. She kept the figurines securely locked. He presumed the delicate looking items were costly. "As you can see, many have been designed as part of a larger Nativity, but not all. Don Quixote's sidekick, Sancho Panza, rode a burro, perhaps much like this one." She pointed to a pot-bellied peasant plopped atop a long-eared donkey. She opened and handed to him a tri-fold, color brochure. "I donate 10 percent of every purchase to The Platero Project. When you get a chance, please check it out."

The man found himself so fascinated by the singular focus of the store's 'livestock,' that he almost forgot his attempt to be discrete, as he mingled with the merchants to whom he'd been told to make deliveries and keep an eye on.

However, in the little than two seconds it took Diane to turn back around, the mystery man was gone as fast as he'd come. She walked to the door and looked out, but there were so many people, he could be anywhere by now. *Oh well*, she thought. *I'll mention it over migas mañana.*

Since she was already at the door, she smiled and did her best to draw passersby inside by handing out brochures like the one she'd given the man. To many a disinterested ear, she talked up the non-profit venture she supported with her sales. When that didn't work, she pulled out the stuffed puppet Jacks and Jennies to capture the attention of the younger crowd. She entertained them with both historical and hysterical tall tales of misadventures from the days of the gold rush. Those that braved entry and made it all the way to the rear of the store, while their moms and dads shopped, were treated to nonstop video loops of who-cares-if-its-unseasonal *Nestor, the Long-Eared Christmas Donkey*.

You can't blame an entrepreneurial woman for trying.

***

"Good afternoon, Señor. Will you be dining alone today?"

The well-dressed man, sporting a coat and tie, nodded in affirmation.

"I have the perfect seat for one, in a quiet alcove with a view. Please, follow me this way."

Delgado showed the man to his table and removed the linen cloth from the plate. He snapped it open and spread it across the man's lap, before handing him a menu. After pouring him a glass of iced water, Delgado assured him his server would be forthcoming.

The man pulled a clean handkerchief from his breast pocket and used it to wipe his glasses, so he could better see in the darkened surroundings. Feigning interest the leather-bound menu, he peered over at the people escorted in, one after the other, in talkative groups. *I'd better act soon.*

From inside his suit jacket—Yes, he wore one even during a swelteringly humid reconnaissance—he carefully removed a long, white envelope on which *Mr. Samuel Delgado, La China Poblana* had been typed. It was the only lettering on the sealed delivery he had been commissioned to make. As the server approached, he slid it back into place in his interior pocket.

"Good afternoon, sir. Can I offer you a drink to accompany your meal today?"

"Thank you, but I'll pass. I'm not sure my boss would appreciate my drinking on the clock."

"Oh, no. Still working? But, it's past five o'clock, time for play now." The young man smiled broadly, flashing brilliantly white teeth in the low dark. Failing to get the desired response, he switched to a more reserved and professional demeanor. "In that case, how about an appetizer while you await your entrée? Do you have any questions about our menu or specials of the day?"

"No. I'm well versed on your offerings," he lied, hoping if later asked, the server would remember this part of the conversation. He noted the server's name tag, *Aiden*. "I will have the *sopa poblana*," he said, then promptly changed his mind. "No, scratch that. It's far too hot out there for soup today, unless it's gazpacho."

The young man's smile returned, although he kept his words in his mouth.

After relooking briefly at the offerings, the man decided. "The *Cecina de Tepeaca* should be enough."

"Excellent choice. With the sides as listed?"

"Yes, as it comes is fine with me." The description of the roasted prickly pear cactus and cured, paprikaless, white sausage made with premium pork loin, garlic, and spices sounded enticing.

"It shouldn't take long, but please let me know if you need anything while you're waiting."

The man determined the best place to leave the envelope, where it was sure to be seen. He stopped another server and asked her where he might find the men's room. She pointed the way, and he stood and walked in that direction. On his return, facing the diners and staff, he discreetly placed the envelope on a shelf below one of the registers. Fortuitous. There was already a small stack of unopened correspondence there. He was able to slide his in the middle of the mail that awaited opening.

With his mission accomplished and unseen, the man returned to his table and awaited his dinner, realizing he was, indeed, famished.

***

Wait. Was that him? The mystery man? Coming out of Delgado's place? With a toothpick in his mouth, no less. Most likely disengaging a lingering culinary disquiet from between his teeth. I watched, as he made his way upstream toward Navarro Street. I looked back at La China Poblana to find Samuel Delgado sneering my way.

I suddenly realized there weren't as many people on the river tonight. The crowd had thinned out. Come to think of it, I hadn't seen my favorite *policía* since...

Chapter Six

OFFICER PAIGE TURNER HAD only recently moved into the charming little Terrell Hills rental with a covered front porch that ran the extend of the house. A lovingly landscaped yard surrounded by privacy fencing, a small back deck, and a detached two-car garage large enough for both her motorcycle and AWD had sealed the deal and promptly put an end to her searching. It was after midnight by the time her watch ended. She returned home, exhausted.

"Oh, Kona. Why does life have to be so complicated?" She scratched behind her friend's ears, a blend of Labrador and Greyhound, she suspected. The stray had chosen Turner as her human and had been her sometimes sole and always soul companion for some six years. Clearly, the massage felt good to the animal. She closed her eyes and nestled into Turner's hands, then pawed at them when the therapeutic fingers slowed or drifted away. Paige laughed. "You like that, huh, girl?" She gave her a few more deep body rubs, before moving toward the door. "Let's get inside before we get eaten up by these blood-thirsty mosquitoes."

The screen door squeaked on rusting hinges, as Paige opened it wide. She reached deep in her pocket for the key and unlocked the wooden sentry, lifting the knob slightly in order to combat its warping. She couldn't wait to get inside and out of her sweat-saturated clothing. Having served to protect her from the burn of the sun, her outerwear and underwear now clung to her body, and not in the nicest of ways.

She filled the old claw tub with water and slowly slid beneath the generous and inviting suds the bath bomb had created, promising herself the indulgent luxury of at least thirty minutes of non-thinking relaxation. Of course, once her body loosened, her thoughts surfaced, and she was no longer in control of their winding and ensnaring ways.

It had been two days already, and two bodies remained unidentified. The only calls in response to the news run, in the local papers and on network television stations, were those made by citizens now hyper-concerned for their own safety amidst tourists in the area of San Antonio's downtown. With the exception of an occasional mugging, when a visitor was heedless enough to stroll the sidewalks all alone, it was usually a peaceful place. From what she'd been told, there'd been no major problems, ever. *Why now?*

They still didn't know how either victim had been killed. The man's death could have been accidental. With that of the woman hot on his heels, it would be quite a coincidence if they weren't somehow intertwined.

She sank deep into the water, until the foam and bubbles covered her shoulders, and steered her thoughts toward more pleasant topics. Of the many people she'd met since moving to the city, Bobbi was the most interesting and personable, by far. The diminutive, yet far from demure, woman exuded a comforting warmth that Turner found she enjoyed being around. She'd walked by Beta's more than a few times and heard Bobbi loudly singing inside the restaurant. Turner smiled, as she wondered how the woman would react when she learned the secret of the tongue that, for now anyway, she was keeping tightly tied.

She allowed her thoughts to linger and wash over her body. After toweling off and pulling on a t-shirt and shorts, she headed to her home office, powered on her laptop, and attempted to do the same with her reluctantly engaging brain.

What am I missing? What is it that I'm not seeing? There has to be something. She pulled out the toxicology reports for at least the tenth time since they had come in earlier in the day and pored over them once more. This time doing a web search of the many unknown pharmacological terms and scanning the paragraphs for insights she may have missed in the first nine go-rounds. Not surprisingly, she found none.

It just didn't make any sense. There were no signs of physical trauma to either victim. Nothing showed on the preliminary drug screens. And, it was obvious that at least the second body had been staged. But why? Was someone trying to keep people away from San Antonio's River Walk? If so, for what reason? *Come on, Paige. Think.* It was no use, her brain was just too tired. She decided to call in a lifeline, who could maybe help her see things in a new light.

"Hi honey. Long time, no hear."

"Hey Mom, and it hasn't been that long. Or have you forgotten my last call?"

"My memory is functioning just fine, dear, but a single day without hearing your voice is like a day without sunshine. If I can't manage to do it on my own, maybe "Whispers of the North" can entice you to come back home. Should I sing it for you?"

Paige laughed heartily, remembering fondly, her mother's love of singing songs of the early '80s. "I'm surprised you didn't just jump right in." For a moment, Paige lingered in the realization that she'd just been thinking about Bobbi's singing, and now... She quickly changed the subject. "You want sunshine; I got plenty of sunshine for you. I'll even throw in triple-digit temperatures as a bonus. But in all seriousness, why don't you sell the house, pack your bags, and come stay for a forever while? Better yet, I'll come and get you. Just say when. I don't like you being there all alone now that Dad's gone."

"Who left whom?" Her mom chuckled. "Now, Paige, you know I'm waiting for you to come to your senses and come back home. I have no intention of moving. I'm here to stay until the good Lord calls me home. Tell me, don't you ever think of moving back to Juneau?"

"Only every single day of every South Texas summer, Mom. You got me on that one."

"I can't imagine why on earth you stay. There are plenty of opportunities in law enforcement here in Alaska. And the men far outnumber the women here."

"Exactly my point, and one of the reasons I had to get away, but I promise to think about it." Paige questioned her mother's remark. Her mother had always seemed okay with her sexuality, so she didn't know what to make of the apparent change. "Despite the fact that I was the first and only female officer assigned to the Sitka station. I was forced to wear outgrown and discarded uniform hand-me-downs. I doubt things have changed." She could now laugh at the memory. At the time, not so much. "Besides, I can't right now. I'm in the middle of an ongoing investigation. Until it's over and done with, I can't get away even for a few days of vacation."

"Well, I'm not going to ask, because ignorance is bliss, and I don't want to know. I prefer to think of my little girl wrapped in the arms of a safe and secure world, as opposed to out there among life's dangerous shadiness. Speaking of, I heard it through the Haines hotline that John Sanders has been asking around about you."

Paige laughed. "Good old John. He must be out of jail and between women again."

"He never gives up. You gotta give him a point for tenacity."

"Yeah well, where I'm concerned, his tenacity is pointless. You know that. We had this discussion years ago. I didn't think we'd ever have to have it again. What's going on, Mom?"

Her mother sighed. "Paige, sweetheart, you know I love and accept you just the way you are. It's just, I want you to be happy. I worry about you, and I miss you, honey."

"Well, I thought you'd be the last person I'd ever have to try to convince that being with a man is no guarantee of a woman's happiness." Her mother's silence was as painful as the memory. "I'm sorry, Mom. I miss you, too." Paige hurriedly changed the subject. "Have you read any good books lately?"

"When have you known me not to read? I seem to be stuck in the mystery genre these days."

As her mother went on to share some of her favorite authors and titles, Paige smiled, remembering the talks and walks she would take with her mother, with no topic unturned and no destination in mind. She had left what she knew as home in order to follow her heart and find herself, only to realize she'd never been lost. Maybe led astray, but not because she was gay. That was more than six years ago. She had since put roots in Texas soil, and with each passing month the possibility of a return to the land of the midnight sun was fading.

Although, she was feeling more homesick these days than she had when she'd first arrived. She remembered it well. The minute she'd sat on Sarah's bed, the tears couldn't be contained. It was as if, all of a sudden, the reality of the miles separating her from her home and mother had hit her. She'd never felt so alone, despite the fact that she was sitting next to someone she thought loved her. She thought she'd at least be in a lasting and long-term, loving relationship. She'd been wrong on both counts. When Paige thought about it, she wasn't sure why she hadn't gone back home when her ill-fated sojourn with Sarah ended. She often felt guilty for leaving her mother all alone in a land that could be so wild and difficult, especially for a woman who was aging, albeit gracefully.

With that thought, Paige prodded, "Do you ever miss Puerto Rico, Mom?"

"No, *hija*. Well, sometimes the language and food, and the music." Her mother always slipped into Spanish when her thoughts and memories returned her to the island where she'd lived most of her life. "I left a lot of bad memories behind in San Juan, where they can stay." She shook off the seeping sadness with a laugh. "Do you remember what it was like when we first moved here to Alaska? You were so young. Philip was transferred in the dead of winter. That phrase meant nothing to us. What did we know? But I loved that man, I would have followed him to the ends of the earth."

"You practically did."

Paige's stepfather, Philip Stoltz, had been a captain in the Coast Guard. The strong and silent, gentle and kind man had been given a choice between Juneau and Miami for relocation. He'd gladly seized the opportunity to get away from the heat of the tropics. He spent his life on the water and reached the rank of rear admiral, before an incurable, stage-four colon cancer sank his ship.

Sometimes, Paige felt that was what she missed the most, the proximity to water. Sure, one could, and many did, make the three-hour drive from San Antonio to the Gulf of Mexico. But the mostly brown water there couldn't compare to the turquoise of the Caribbean or the deep blue of the Pacific Ocean. Too many of the Texas creeks were dry beds filled with deep cracks crying for a much-needed rain.

She found herself yearning for the sounds of the large bodies of water and their craft. From the hoisting of a small sloop's sail and the smell of salt in the air, to the lapping of continuous, rolling waves as they landed on shore, the memories had a strong pull on her emotions. She'd swapped her bathing suit for a jacket and learned to love the rocky beaches, even preferred the cool, refreshing winds of the north over the sand and relentless sun south of the mid-Atlantic. Despite the beauty of the tropics, her heart's compass would always work to pull her north, leaving her wondering just why she stayed in Texas. It was a question she was asking herself more and more these days.

She missed the natural beauty of the far northern state, where she'd been lovingly raised. She'd adventured on float planes and sea kayaks, with the excitement of seeing pods of orca and humpback whales in the wild. She'd had the privilege of seeing grizzlies in full color. Not on a magazine's page, but through a binoculars' lens on Kodiak Island. The most important years of her life were spent in a place where moose grazed, bald eagles soared, and salmon came to spawn. She was growing terribly nostalgic as a result of this call. "I promise to give it some thought, Mom."

"Well, at least come to visit. I'm not getting any younger, you know."

And, there it was. The most painful thrust to her heart. Not that her mother meant for the plea to hurt her so. After their goodbyes, as she always did, Paige turned to music in an attempt to extend their time together. Certain songs reminded her of her mother. As she turned on the tunes, she reached for her brush. She didn't have her mother's talent, but found art calming, meditative even. Painting made her feel closer to her mother, who first taught Paige the transformative magic of the canvas.

As she stroked the bristles of her brush across the palette and onto the cloth, she enjoyed the melodies of one of her mother's favorite *puertorriqueños*, Marc Anthony. "You sang to me," Paige murmured, yet unaware that she was creating an image that closely resembled a certain someone who had recently claimed space in her subconscious.

When Marc Anthony gave way to Luis Miguel's "Cómplices," Paige paused. Few people knew that the Mexican singer had been born to a Spanish father and Italian mother in San Juan. He was one of her mother's favorites. Paige thought about the words of the song. What could she say? Every sunrise held promise. Crime solving and romance could be her new reality.

Chapter Seven

THE REALITY AT BETA'S was that I hadn't received anywhere near the number of reservations I had anticipated for Mother's Day. I held onto hope that I'd be surprised by a large number of walk-ins. Either way, I refused to let anything dampen my spirit or weaken the energy with which I always celebrated this day. I'd had a late night, followed by an early morning preparing the tamales that had become my tradition for the day, especially the hard-to-come-by sweet tamales. I colored mine pink and in some of the steamed husks added raisins, pineapple, coconut, and cream to the masa in varying combinations. On the spicy side, I offered *tamales de rajas con queso* alongside the more traditional beef, pork, and chicken that my returning regulars always requested, even outside of the holidays.

Normally, on a special occasion like today, I wouldn't have a minute to take a load off far into the evening. This year, the opposite was true. A minute out of every hour was about all I was needed. It was heartbreaking.

I was certain the decrease in the number of mothers present had nothing to do with a decline in children celebrating those who had brought them into this world or nurtured them. I expected they were just doing it elsewhere, in a place that hadn't been so tainted of late. Oh well, I hoped for a better turnout on Tuesday for *el Día de las Madres*, the traditional day on which Mexicans celebrated their mothers and all others who had taken on those responsibilities.

I was cleaning and preparing to call it a night, when I sensed a presence enter the restaurant from behind me.

"Happy Mom's Day!"

"Rachel! Oh Rachel, *mijita*."

We locked in a long and loving embrace. I was overwhelmed with good emotions upon seeing the young woman I'd helped raise through her troubling early teen years and into the young woman she'd become.

"It's been so long, Rachel. How are you? How have you been?" I pulled a chair out. "Please sit. I've missed you, honey."

"It's been good. Thanks to you, Moms."

My heart filled with love at the sound of the familiar nickname Rachel had chosen for me as her other mother all those years ago.

"Don't think I don't know that it's been you who's been funding my college education and loading my account so I can pay for books and dining room fees each semester. It sure hasn't been Mom. Did you know she's gone to Kentucky now? I'm not sure when, or if, she'll ever settle. She just has no clue what she wants."

As if suddenly remembering the purpose of her visit, she opened her purse and took out a tiny gift bag. "I got you something. I hope you like it." She held it out to me, and I smiled as I separated the shredded tissue paper inside the bag to find a small box. I opened it to see a silver charm nestled in cotton. "I love it. Mostly because it's from you. You know I would love anything you give to me, simply because you chose it."

Rachel laughed. "Yeah. I know. I bet you still have those horrible school art projects I brought home."

"Now, don't go dissin' my favorite mini pinch and coil pots. They are works of heart that the finest professional clay throwers could never replace." I looked again at the piece of jewelry. "Knowing you, there must be some hidden meaning to the design."

"You always did know me so well." Rachel smiled. The craftsman, or more likely craftswoman, who designed it had imagined what the letters that spell out *I LOVE YOU MOMS* would look like if they were laid one on top of the other into that little square charm. "Dope, huh?"

"It's special and unique, that's for sure. And I love it."

"I chose it because it's different and special, like you." Rachel looked at me with tears threatening to spill from her eyes. "I miss you, Bobbi. You were the best thing that ever happened to me and Mom."

I couldn't hold it in any longer. I didn't even try. I wrapped Rachel in a long hug. When I'd composed myself enough to speak again, I reminded her, "You do know that just because your mother and I didn't work out doesn't mean that you and I can't still have the same relationship we had, right?"

Rachel tightened her lips and nodded, as her tears freely flowed.

"So, where are you staying, with your mother gone and school being out?"

"I've been hanging with different friends, moving around, not wanting to impose on anyone."

"Oh Rachel. Why didn't you call me or come see me sooner? You know you'll always have a home with me, don't you? I mean, I can't offer you a princess's palace, but you're always welcome. I want us to talk about this seriously, and soon. Promise?"

Rachel nodded again and wiped her tears with a proffered napkin.

***

Despite the fact that she didn't get much sleep, Turner was out the door early and filled with hopeful energy. On her days off, she liked to help out in what she thought of as her community, so she dressed to help serve the homeless and working poor at St. Benedict's, not far from the river.

As she made her way to the cafeteria-style serving station, she nearly collided with a Seguin Park resident, who was hurriedly making his way in from the opposite direction.

Mark's stomach was growling, and he was looking forward to his first real meal of the day. He was also anxious to show his bench buddies what he'd found on the front page. If that newspaper hadn't been discarded on his slatted sleeping space, they might never have known what happened to poor Lenny.

The starving vagrant moved through the line rapidly and exited with a plate filled with seasoned beef, mashed potatoes, green beans, and stewed tomatoes. Better than he'd eaten in days. He moved toward a table with some familiar, haggard-looking faces. It was hot out there. Everybody was suffering.

Claiming his place, he set his plate beside the folded newspaper and went to get some water from the cooler at the front table. When he returned, the men acknowledged him as an acquaintance. One of them asked, "Hey, what's that you got there?"

"Yesterday's newspaper. Someone left it by my bench," Mark answered around a mouthful of vegetables.

The photograph couldn't be missed. It nearly filled the entire top fold of The Sentinel.

"Lemme see it," the man commanded, as he reached across the table.

Mark handed it over, eager to share his discovery.

"Praise Jesus," the man exclaimed loudly and quickly looked away from the picture. "That looks like Lenny. I haven't seen him for a few days. You guys know him?" He was happy to pass the paper along. A few of the guys confirmed they'd seen him around, but no one seemed to know him well, par for their ever-transient and invisible population.

"What's this about?" Al exclaimed. "He was found dead? My sweet Lord!" At that realization, he tossed the paper back to Mark as if it were covered in something contagious and shook his head in dismay. "This world is one fucked-up place."

Soon, the news story and paper were largely forgotten, as the men focused on their eating.

***

When the place had cleared out, Turner traded her serving apron in for a bucket of soapy water and gloves and set about cleaning tables. She saw the newspaper where it had been left, and her heart may have skipped a tiny beat. *Is it coincidence? Or a message?* She quickly looked around at the few remaining faces. None of them seemed to be watching or the least bit interested. She doubted any of them had sat at this table. Still, she snagged the paper and carried it over to those still seated.

"Hello gentlemen. Please forgive this interruption while you're eating, but did any of you happen to see who was sitting over there?" She pointed to the empty table.

"I didn't. Did any of you?" One of them looked at all the others. Unfortunately, no one had seen. The unheard conversation from earlier was on the verge of being repeated.

"What's that you got there?" The lead speaker prompted, pointing to the paper.

"It's a newspaper someone left behind."

"Hey, that looks like Lenny. Guys, what do you think?"

The others looked at the paper and nodded in agreement.

"Sure does. What kind of trouble is that man in now?"

Turner's expression turned somber. "I'm sorry if he was a friend of yours. Actually, I'm sorry regardless of whether you knew him or not."

"He dead?"

Turner solemnly nodded. "Yes, sadly. His body was found in the San Antonio River the day before yesterday. You say his name was Lenny? Leonard maybe? Do any of you know his last name? Or where he might have lived?"

"Don't know anything more than Lenny. He lived with us for the last few weeks over Seguin Park way."

Realizing nothing more was forthcoming, she excused herself. "Thank you, fellows. I'm so sorry to have brought you this bad news. Please take your time eating." She went back to her cleaning but couldn't wait to finish and pay Seguin Park a visit.

Night was falling, and the corner of Pecan and Navarro Streets was not exactly where Turner wanted to be, especially out of uniform and lacking her gun belt. She did see a few of her colleagues patrolling the streets, so onward she marched to an area that was largely avoided after sunset by all those familiar with the place.

She could see that almost every bench was already occupied by a huddled body, and could only hope all of them were still living and breathing. As she neared each wooden bed, she recognized a few now-shadowed faces of the men and women she'd served dinner to, just an hour or so earlier.

Without her cop clothes on, she was a target for the catcalls and unwanted attention aimed her way.

"Hey pretty lady," a man sneered, as he entered her personal space. "What's a nice girl like you doing in this seedy-ass place?" His toothless grin spread wide, as he cackled at his own joke before passing her by and walking to what she assumed would be his resting place for the evening. She decided maybe it would help if she pulled her badge out and was sorry she didn't have a flashlight. Her phone's light would work to a certain degree. She approached the bench dwellers one by one, showing them the newspaper article and photograph. Once they saw her badge, most of them didn't even bother to look at the photo, yet claimed they'd, "Never seen the dude." She finally stumbled upon Mark.

"Yeah, I knew him, well, I knew who he was. Lenny was his name."

"Do you happen to know his last name?"

He looked at her with wide eyes before smiling the biggest smile she'd ever seen. "Fraid not. This environment ain't exactly that kinda place."

She looked over to the transit hub. Suddenly, she got an idea. "Can you hang out here for just a few more minutes? I have another photograph I want to show you."

He laughed. "Lady, where else would I be going? This is it for me."

Turner felt foolishly oblivious of the plight of the homeless, as the man stretched out on his bench. She turned and walked quickly away to where she thought a news box might be. The first one, of course, was broken, the second completely empty. The dead bodies were helping the floundering print media sell like hotcakes. Finally, some six blocks away, she happened upon a little mom and pop store. The man at the counter had the paper open, reading it.

She showed her badge before bargaining, "Can I buy that from you? I need it for official police business."

He pushed his glasses higher on his nose, gave her a blank stare, and handed it to her. He waved away her payment.

She nearly ran back the way she'd come, until she reached Mark's bench in the park, where she hurriedly showed him the front page of the morning paper.

"Holy shit! Should I be worried?" He blanched and his eyes grew huge, as he learned there had been another body found. He looked to her with what seemed like genuine concern for his own safety. With both the hanging and shaking of his head, he let her know that he'd already answered his own rhetorical inquiry.

"I take it you knew her, too?"

"Yes. Yes, of course. She was one of us, too. Sheila was her name."

"I don't suppose, you happen to know *her* last name?"

"Nope. Sorry. That's all I got for you, Officer." Mark took his eyes off the paper and looked at her again. His expression changed. "Hey. Wait a minute. Didn't I see you earlier, at St. Benedict's?"

"Yes, I was there." She didn't know what to make of the silence that seemed to separate them and stretch for an eternity. She filled the void with a simple, "Thank you, Mark, for your time, willingness to be of assistance, and the information."

"Glad I could help."

Turner walked back toward the patrol car that would take her to the station. Before she rounded the corner, she looked back one last time. Mark had already stretched back out on the wooden slats of the park bench. She couldn't imagine he could be comfortable or would have a restful sleep. In their world, she assumed it was best for them to sleep with one eye open at all times, but especially now.

***

As soon as the obvious, plain-clothes officer was out of sight, Derek Flynn swooped in to see what information twenty dollars would buy. He thought he'd hit the jackpot with his first headline of the night, but before the rolling of the presses, he would have cause to stop them with an amendment. He quickly jotted the information in his pad and made a beeline for the office.

"Hey man," he called to Jameson in an attempt to be heard over the music blasting at his desk. It took an invasion of the man's personal space and a shaking of his cubicle's walls to get his attention.

"What? I can't hear you. Louder Huckleberry Newshound." Jameson quirked the side of his mouth before sneering defiantly in Flynn's direction.

Flynn roared, "Turn. It. Down!"

Jameson heard him that time. Everyone in the newsroom did. Jameson reached to lower the volume, but only a notch.

"I can't even think, let alone put a story together, with all that noise." Flynn gestured toward the monitor's screen that clearly showed the volume still nearly as high as it would go.

The boss man, Edwards, came out of his office to see what all the commotion was about.

"Chill, little man," Jameson whispered to Flynn and muted the sound.

"Now is as good a time as any to address the matter," Edwards announced. "Jameson, you've got to stop with the music. When you're here late at night or early in the morning by yourself, that's one thing, but Derek here is not the first person to express an inability to concentrate when it's so loud. Get yourself some headphones if you want to listen to music at work."

"Yes, sir," Jameson pulled a pair of headphones from his drawer.

Flynn shook his head and walked back to his cubicle, upset over the interaction that had just occurred, and for what? Nothing. The man already had what he needed to keep from distracting others. And sure, Flynn had caught the slur Jameson hurled his way, the one that likened him to a cartoon character with a southern drawl. So what if he was from Mississippi and did still speak with a little accent? Jameson was so marginalized, he alienated everyone. It wasn't even that they didn't have similar tastes in music. Flynn never listened to his while writing, nor did he bust out windows with the volume. He looked at his reflection in the mirror by his desk and found it ironic. By appearance alone, anyone might think his and Jameson's personalities were mismatched. Flynn was the one with a few tattoos and piercings, and shoulder-length, straight, brown hair. Women he dated described him as having dark, brooding, bad-boy good looks. It just goes to show that appearances can be deceiving. Anyway, now that the reverb in his head had gone, maybe he could get to work.

Flynn watched Jameson storm off, apparently taking his anger for a walk.

***

As I was sweeping and preparing to close for the night, I noticed a suspicious prowler strolling my way along the riverfront. I stilled the scratching of my broom against the floor's tile and stood to watch his stealthy approach. Apparently, he didn't see. He was taking his time, stopping here and there. It appeared he was scoping out the businesses to see which ones had open doors for easier entry. As he neared my pub, I backed further inside. Surprisingly, given recent circumstances, I was not feeling at all afraid. I just wanted to see if he'd walk by or dare cross my darkened threshold. He stopped at my entrance, his nose sniffing in the air, before his decision was made.

"Hey boy," I called to him.

He looked at me and his tail set to wagging, cautiously yet excitedly.

"You hungry? I'm sure I've got some scraps you can have. Come on in and hang out with me for a while."

The brown and black stray quickly lapped at the water bowl I'd set on the floor, while I tossed some of the day's leftover ground beef into the microwave so the heat would release the meat's flavor. He looked toward the kitchen as the smell permeated the atmosphere, and whined in anticipation as I plated his dinner.

"Here you go, boy. Oh, excuse me, I see you're a girl. I'm sorry. My bad for not looking closer. Happens to me all the time, chica. Believe me, I understand completely."

I watched her scarf down the meat, wondering how long it'd been since she'd eaten.

"*Pobrecita*," I stooped to collect the plate she'd licked clean and reached to give her back a rigorous rub. "Where'd you come from?"

She stayed with me, as I finished cleaning and closed my cantina, and afterward followed me to my truck. "I guess it can't hurt these days to have an escort." Fully expecting we'd say our goodbyes at my unlocked and opened driver's door, I found myself saddened by her forlorn expression. Her frown turned upside down when I invited, "Well, come on. Get in." Without hesitation, she jumped onto my old truck's busting-at-the seams seat.

"Surely, you must belong to someone?" I mused aloud as we drove home. "No tag. No collar. I'll check to see if you're chipped in the morning. For tonight, I guess you're crashing with me."

I swear she smiled at me. She gave her tail one thunderously happy thump. Who was I kidding? I was equally happy to have some company, if only for a little while.

Chapter Eight

NEEDLESS TO SAY, MY newfound canine companion and I rolled in a little later than usual on Monday morning. As I suspected, there was no easy way for me to find this sweetie's human. I figured I'd let fate decide her future, all the while knowing I was already getting attached to my four-legged amiga.

A part of my routine I was quickly coming to dread, was to stoop and pick up the newspaper standing sentinel at my door. I slid the rubber band off and unrolled the paper.

TWO BODIES ID'd AS TWO MORE FOUND ON RIVER WALK

"No fucking way!" I barked my incredulity and startled the girl at my feet. I patted her furry head. "Sorry, but this is getting out of control." I'm not sure why I felt the need to explain the reason the expletive had escaped my previously nonparental potty mouth to a dog. *Is that how it's going to be from now on?*

I set the coffee pot percolating. What can I say? My place is old school. I watched, as the dog claimed a spot in the kitchen and curled there quietly. "Well, okay then," I responded with a smile in my heart and on my face.

As I waited for my brew to bubble, I read the article. This time there was not one, but two bodies. A supposed couple had been found dead on the river's heart-shaped Marriage Island.

When is this going to end? What in hell is going on? I read the rest of the story.

The bodies from the days before had been identified, but only with first names. They were recognized by a few members of a nearby homeless community and volunteers that had served them at either the soup kitchen or one of the downtown shelters. The deceased had been homeless.

Who on earth would want to kill people already so down on their luck? Robbery certainly couldn't have been a motive. And had they been moved to where they'd been found? Were the scenes staged? What did it all mean? My mind was abuzz with wonderment, as the lid of the coffee pot rattled and gurgled, gently lifting as it blew off some steam. Yes, let's add a little caffeine to the mix of my hypervolatile emotions.

I took the largest cup I had and filled it to the brim, before sitting back in the chair and taking a tongue scalding sip. It was hotter than hell, but I couldn't wait. I needed a jump-starting jolt coursing through my veins.

Soon after, Diane and Charlie made appearances. Over *chilaquiles* and coffee, our regular morning meeting of mouths and minds got underway without delay.

Diane always wore her heart on her sleeve. "*Pobrecitos*, all they have are first names for these *desgraciados*. The police will probably never know where they're from or find their families."

Charlie chimed in, "Apparently, neither had ever even been charged with loitering or vagrancy, so there are no fingerprints to help out that way."

I don't know if I spoke my thoughts out loud or merely to myself, but *ain't nobody got time for that shit these days*. San Antonio cops are far too busy with more serious crime to persecute such victims of society by incarcerating them in jails already overburdened with the likes of more dangerous criminals. As long as they were just hanging out and not hurting anybody, they were left alone. Or were they? The causes and motives for these deaths had yet to be determined. No one had a clue who was dropping the bodies, or how the victims were being selected.

I decided to confess my doubts. "You all know I've never trusted Delgado. And I still say there's something suspicious about his untimely and supposedly coincidental disappearance, right before such a busy week in the restaurant world, precisely before all of this got under way."

Diane always shied away from speaking badly about another. "We know, Bobbi. I just don't know that I'm ready to sentence and hang Samuel, yet. After all, he was once one of us."

"Let's think about this rationally and objectively for a minute. Who would have a reason, a motive, to kill homeless people? And, why? Why pile them exclusively along this particular stretch of the river? There has to be a reason."

We stayed silent for a few minutes, each exploring our innermost thoughts, until I couldn't bite my tongue anymore and got the wrecking ball swinging. "My money's still on Delgado. I mean, look at what he did to those poor river ducks that were unfortunate enough to swim his restaurant's way."

"You know, you might be on to something."

Diane put her head in her hands, still shaking it. "*Por el amor de Dios.* Don't encourage her, Charlie."

"I wasn't referring to the woebegone waterfowl, or to Sam at all for that matter. Bobbi, when you said, 'My money's on Delgado,' it made me think about placing bets, gambling, and that triggered a memory. Do you all remember that, every year, someone in some office picks up the gambling gauntlet and tries to push through a bill that would allow casinos to operate in Texas?"

"That's right. And those of us who like to indulge in such a vice from time to time always read that news with interest and hope, forgetting that it'll never happen as long as the deciding vote continues to be cast by one man in Austin, whom I refuse to name."

"Meanwhile, we, like every other Texan who enjoys a playcation, continue to take our money out of state or to our one and only tribally run slots and cards place. Do you remember the last time it was in the news? There was mention of some casino owner with high hopes of opening a dice and wheel joint right here on the river."

"Ha. Fat chance of that happening, even if it were to be allowed. There's not enough available space anywhere here. Whether we realize it or not, we're sitting on some primo property, or at least we were, once upon a pre-Cinco-de-Mayo time."

"My point exactly. Maybe Mr. Money Bags was hoping to make business go so far south for us, we'd all be ready and willing to sell our places."

All ears perked up at that, and all minds appeared to excitedly engage in speculation.

"Hey, I almost forgot to ask," Charlie interrupted my thoughts, "have either of you noticed a well-dressed man, completely out of his less-than-elegant element these last few days? An older man, not completely gray like me"—Charlie smiled at the self-comparison—"but definitely with more salt than pepper in his hair and goatee."

"I had a customer that sounds like it could have been him, just yesterday. I found him looking at my ass during our after-dinner slow time." Diane paused there, I suspected for dramatic reasons. "You know, the big one I keep at the front of the store." Neither one of us missed the glint in her eye or the upward quirk of her salaciously speaking mouth.

Suddenly, I remembered. Not her ass, the man's appearance.

"As a matter of fact, I did see a man like that. Twice. He was here Thursday with the crowd in the evening, and I saw him again yesterday, leaving Delgado's restaurant."

Hmmm. What, if anything, could it mean? Who could he be? If he was trying to be sneaky, why in the hell did he dress like that? Surely he had to know he was drawing attention to himself. Could that be what he wanted?

"That would explain why we've all recently received buyout offers," Charlie said.

"Perhaps the mystery man was the postal carrier. Regardless of whoever and why, how sad that anyone could find the lives of the homeless so dispensable," Diane fretted.

"Maybe he didn't so much choose his victims because they were homeless as much as because their homelessness provided a much-needed opportunity. Think about it. Who would even notice or report them missing?"

As we quietly contemplated the graying mystery man, our thoughts were interrupted by the arrival of my favorite enforcer of the law.

"Hello everyone," she greeted us. "How fortunate for me. I can speak with all three of you at once." Turner smiled, and my heart went thump-a-thump. I hoped the others couldn't see the force of it beat beneath my floral embroidered, white poplin shirt.

Coincidentally, I'd braided my long raven hair, just for the possible and hoped for occasion. I found myself wondering if the focus of my overactive imagination would notice the slight hint of eye shadow, rouge, and lipstick I'd taken the effort to apply. I almost always left my face natural. Even Kacie—Yes, I was already thinking of the dog as my own, and thus had given her a name—peered around the corner. She may have been in search of more food, or perhaps she'd detected the faintest aroma of some foolish pheromone I was exuding.

"Officer Turner," I stammered invitingly in her direction, "please join us for some breakfast."

Apparently, she found me, or at least my offering, irresistibly tempting. Her eyes sparkled and her smile reached my way. "I must say, it sure does look and smell delicious."

Thankfully, I'd cooked some extra.

When I returned with her plate, I pulled out a chair and sat by her side. "I hope you like them. Here you go." I passed her some warm tortillas, and she immediately dug in.

"Mmmm. This is so good." She looked at me, and my heart melted like the cheese covering the eggs on her plate. What could I do but smile and drool like a fool as I gazed in her direction?

"As I was saying," Diane continued, "we talked for a while about my store and merchandise, but it was strange how he appeared and disappeared so quietly and quickly. In the blink of an eye and the middle of a sentence—*poof*—he was gone."

I filled Turner in on the cloak-and-dagger comings and goings of the stranger. "It's the same man I mentioned to you the other day."

She nodded, letting me know she remembered. "I'm sure you've all seen today's news?" Her face fell. "I don't know how that information leaked to the press. I didn't want the fact that we'd identified the bodies to get out."

"Why?" Diane questioned in earnest.

Turner sighed. "Because now the killer knows that we'll be watching the park. He won't go back there for his victims, assuming that's where he'd been getting them. He probably won't single out any of the nearby encampments, in fear that we'll have undercovers in all of them. We might have had a chance if we'd been able to keep that detail under wraps."

"Any idea how it got out?"

"None."

"Speaking of detail, have the causes of death been determined?"

"We're still waiting on some results, but there were no signs of trauma to either body. No blood, no bruising, no evidence of any known drugs in their system. I'm not a forensic scientist, but it just doesn't make sense."

"Perhaps they were poisoned?" Charlie suggested. "Maybe I've read too many cozy mysteries, but it does seem a popular way to kill someone. It's relatively invisible and nonviolent."

"And now with the couple found on Marriage Island, he's managed to kill two at once. Maybe they didn't even know each other?" I stirred the thickening stew in our collective brains' pot. Toil and trouble, our black cauldron bubbled. "They were found by a geocacher out doing some predawn treasure hunting, were they not?"

Turner confirmed my belief. "Unfortunately, I doubt the young man who found them was looking for anything remotely close to what he found. We can't seem to catch a break in the investigation. Whoever our culprit is, he or she doesn't seem to have accomplished their goal yet."

For her part, Turner took notes on the description of the mystery man. She appeared to consider our offer of a surreptitious stakeout, before ultimately dismissing it as too dangerous. So much for my chance to play undercover cop. Oh well, I'd rather play under the covers with a certain cop, anyway. *WTF? There I go again.* Thankfully, it was time for all of us to toss in the tortillas and prepare for the coming day.

Before we went our separate ways, we voiced our concerns about how badly these murders might affect our businesses. They already seemed to be suffering.

Charlie was the first to admit, "My sales are definitely dropping. I don't have near the number of book browsers. Only the most daring and intrepid readers visit me these days." Apparently inspired by the bookseller's open and honest sharing, Di too, spoke of her retail slump. Personally, I tried not to think about it much. It was simply too defeating and depressing.

Alone again, I reached for my trusted stereo's selection knob and switched from CD to FM stereo, in search of my favorite station, Radio Lobo. I was desperately in need of the wolf's howling and the comforting old-school songs I could relate to. While I enjoyed contemporary hits, my heart would always belong to days gone by and the decades that retained some wonderful memories.

El Paso born Vikki Carr sang *"Mala Suerte"* like she understood where I was coming from. I scraped what little leftovers there were onto a plate I'd already designated as the dog's and carried it into the kitchen. Kacie was such a good girl; no one had seen hide nor hair of her during our extended morning talk. Suddenly feeling guilty, I logged on to the laptop I carried with me and checked the local lost and found for missing pets.

I was relieved to find there weren't any that seemed to match this little min-pin, or could she be a diminutive Doberman? I didn't care if she was a Heinz 57. She appeared to be content with me, so I concluded that I wouldn't exhaust myself in a search for someone who couldn't be bothered to scour the city for my little bi-color pup.

The door was always open. She could go the same way she had come. As for her name, I'd chosen it after deciding her fur was the same color as my favorite barbecue sauce. When I later looked in a dictionary, I found a deeper meaning. Who knew Kacie could mean alert and vigilant? Maybe she'd been sent by an angel above to watch over me during this time of trouble.

***

Turner did her best to put herself in the mind of a killer, who, for whatever reason, was pulling his victims from the homeless population. Knowing little more than that, she searched her brain for another plausible place where he might recruit the downtrodden. *God knows, there are many unfortunate souls out there.* Those she served at St. Benedict's were only a tiny fraction. San Antonio was the nation's seventh largest city. As she made her rounds, cautioning all the street people she came upon to be extra vigilant until this villain was caught, she got an idea. She decided to go directly to the source, Seguin Park, for her information.

"Let me ask you guys something. If this park were unavailable to you, I'm not saying that it is, but if it were, where would you go?"

"Back to the bridge," one of them answered without hesitation.

Of course. The bridges offered shelter from the elements. In the heat of the summer, however, being tucked under all that concrete and asphalt would have to be inhumanely unbearable. Still, she knew the bridges were home to fairly large communities of homeless. Off to San Pedro she trotted.

Naturally, as soon as she showed face and uniform, the squatters scrambled to gather their belongings and disappear, fearing a pending eviction. Recognizing she'd likely get her most useful information from the more fearless of the bunch, she focused on those who staked a rightful claim to their turf. "Hi there," she greeted a middle-aged man who'd just taken a seat on the lopsided cushion in the middle of a torn and tattered old sofa. She held out a hand. "I'm not here to take you in or run you off. I'm just here to ask a few questions. We're looking for a man who seems to be targeting the homeless."

The man, who'd readied himself to rise, settled back into what was left of the foam. "We know about the bodies."

"Have you seen or heard about anyone, not a police officer, but anyone who, maybe, looks like they don't belong? Anyone asking questions or trying to get someone to do some work for them? Anything like that at all?"

The man scratched at the scruffy hair on his chin and thought for a while. "You mean other than the regulars that come looking for fools to make some dope drops?"

"Yes. This would likely be someone new. Although, I guess he could also be involved with drugs." Turner felt so ineffectual, having so little to go on.

The man slowly shook his head. "I can't think of anyone right now."

She handed him a sandwich and a bottle of water for his time and information. "I'll be back. Please tell your friends to be on the lookout and let me know if you hear of anyone or anything."

***

Flynn straightened his tie and smoothed his shirt front. He steeled his nerves and walked toward Jameson's cubicle. Thankfully, he was there, headphones on and looking out the window at the park below. He seemed to be thinking about something important. Flynn intentionally made noise as he approached, hoping to announce his arrival and not appear to be sneaking up on him. The day was more bright than gray, and the window didn't offer a reflection of his approach. He reached out and tapped Jameson on the shoulder.

Jameson turned and looked at him before removing the headphones. The music was so loud, Flynn suspected the man would be deaf before he reached his thirtieth birthday. Instead of turning the sound off, Jameson pulled out his desk drawer and stuck his dual speakers inside.

"Hey man, listen, I'm sorry about the other day."

With a sly smile and an unreadable expression Jameson responded, "No worries. Today's a new day." He spun his chair back around and resumed his neighborhood watch.

While Flynn wasn't sure what he'd expected, it certainly wasn't a peaceful exchange with the man who'd gone ballistic during their last verbal confrontation.

Apparently sensing he hadn't left, Jameson turned back around and waited for Flynn to finish what he wanted to say.

"The irony is that I listen to the same kind of music. Just not so loud, or when I'm working, trying to write." Flynn held something out to him. "Consider it a peace offering." Jameson looked at him before reaching to take what he held in his hand. Flynn handed over a ticket to an upcoming Seether concert, with backstage passes for a meet and greet at the Aztec Theatre.

"How in the hell did you score these?" Jameson's eyes grew as big as saucers. "I've been trying to get tickets ever since the tour was announced months ago. I couldn't even get an overpriced, scalped, near-nosebleed seat."

Flynn smiled. "Let's just say I know some people."

"Apparently." Jameson laughed.

"I got one for myself, too. So, we'll be sitting together. I hope that won't be a problem?"

Jameson smiled and put out his hand for a shake. "Apology accepted man, but you didn't have to go to such an extreme."

Mission accomplished, Flynn returned to his desk and resumed working on his story.

Chapter Nine

UNLIKE KEVIN JAMESON'S, DEREK Flynn's family had always been supportive and proud of their son's accomplishments, no matter how small. Upon seeing his byline on the front page for the first time, his mother had called and invited him to dinner to celebrate. Not that she'd be cooking. She had turned that domestic drudgery over to a personal chef long ago. He'd be meeting them at The Grill at Leon Springs, where the Dominion crowd liked to dine.

He was late, but only by a few intentional minutes. He couldn't stand the preseating small talk. Still, he apologized as he put his hand on his father's Armani-clad shoulder and bent over his mother's for his customary peck on her cheek. She was dressed to the nines. He could only imagine how much her entire ensemble had cost. In jeans and a plain t-shirt, he felt a trifle underdressed. At least he had taken the time to throw on a sports jacket.

"Here dear, before I forget." His mother handed him a stack of gift cards to multiple high-end restaurants downtown. Although her CEO husband more than provided for her needs, she sold wine to keep herself occupied and was often given such perks.

"Thanks, Mom." He was given them so often; it had become a chore to use them. He reluctantly tucked them inside his bulging wallet.

She followed the gesture with a suggestion, "After we order, you can tell us all about your trending rise to fame."

His father chose the Chilean sea bass "Malaysian style," and his mother the panko crusted Alaskan halibut. Derek was torn between two entrées. He ultimately passed on the pan seared, jumbo sea scallops with truffle nage and decided to go with the barbecued, stuffed quail with cheddar cheese and jalapeño sausage.

"And bring us a bottle of your Domaine du Chateau de Meursault 'Meursault du Chateau' Blanc," his father added.

"An excellent selection, sir."

"For now, that will be all."

The server bowed slightly and took his leave of the table.

"I've been bragging to all my golfing partners about my son, the journalist, whose stories are front and center on The Sentinel's lead page these days. We're all waiting to see what we'll read from you next," the elder Flynn said.

Derek reached for a piece of flatbread and spooned a little hummus aside the stuffed jalapeño he'd already appropriated from the assortment of tapas. The appetizers had apparently been ordered before he arrived. Using that action as a buffer, he searched for the words to set his father straight.

"Yeah, well don't hold your breath, Dad. Remember, I'm a crime reporter. Unless the crime is of an extremely sensational nature, my writing isn't likely to make the front page on a regular basis. So, you might want to put your boasting and bragging to the Dominion Country Club boys on hold. It's not like I control the nature of the crimes that take place. I just write about them after they've been committed."

Once out there on the table, reality was quickly and ceremoniously brushed aside by their plates as they arrived. They drained the bottle of indulgent wine, right before they started in on the apple crepia and coffee. Derek remarked on the abrupt and unusual change in his father's demeanor.

"You've become quiet this evening, Dad. Are you disappointed in me? It seems the cat got your tongue right after I suggested you not grow too accustomed to seeing my byline on the front page."

"I'm sorry, Derek. My mood had, has, nothing to do with that, I assure you. The timing was purely coincidental. I regret I've allowed some of today's business problems have an effect on me this evening. You know I'm proud of you. Your Mother and I both are. And we support you in whatever you do. Did I hear you hint at a burgeoning awareness that serving as a staff writer may not be what you want for a long-term career, anyway. Did I imagine that?" Michael Flynn smiled his son's way.

"I don't know if I said it, Dad. But you're right. I have been thinking it. I just don't seem to be going anywhere with what I'm doing. The problem is, I don't know what else I'd do. I haven't had much time, lately, to think about it."

"It doesn't have anything to do with money does it? How's your financial situation? Do you need any?"

Derek couldn't help but laugh at the inquiry. "You're kidding me, right? I mean, you already pay my rent and utilities, and you just gave me a new car. Luckily, I was able to talk you out of buying a condo at La Cascada. The sky is always the limit with you, Dad."

His father smiled. He was proud of his place in life and all that it allowed him to do. "Are you expecting me to believe you'd rather I tossed you out to fend for yourself and have you live in some roach-infested hovel filled with second-or-third-hand furniture you found at some garage sale?"

Though he was no connoisseur of fine wine, Derek honestly couldn't taste the difference between the $200 bottle they'd shared, and what he drank with friends over a casual dinner at 10 percent of that. He put his glass on the table. "Of course not. I'm extremely grateful."

"You're my only son, Derek. Our only child. That's what parents do. Help you out as you leave home and set out on your own. My parents did it for me. It's a Flynn legacy."

The men raised the dregs in their glasses as a toast, while Mrs. Flynn drank water silently.

***

On the other side of the railroad tracks, Jameson lived a different reality. He'd had roommates from time to time but found he couldn't stand sharing his space, so they were short lived and few and far between. He made do with what he could afford, which currently was an old and ill-maintained studio with peeling paint, a mini fridge, and a hot plate. With no money for a car, he walked, rode his bike, or utilized VIA's public transportation. He was mad at the world and his parents for so forsaking him, but most of all at himself for enduring the limitations on a life that he himself had created. At least he was beholden to no one. He owed no one but his landlord and CPS Electric monthly. For that, he was grateful.

From his office window, he often looked down on the people that called Seguin Park home. He knew he was only one notch above their station. He had a job. That was all that separated him from their fate. He'd done a lot of research into the plight of the homeless and realized that, statistically, many suffered from mental health problems and drug addictions. Which came first, the chicken or the egg? Regardless, it was a difficult cycle to break.

***

As the sun rose on a new day, many San Antonians wondered if it would be another Day of the Dead. One person had reason to hope that wouldn't be the case. "I wanted people scared, not dead. Jesus Christ!" The man ran trembling fingers through well-gelled hair that resisted control and continuously fell forward onto his forehead. Likely a product of profuse sweating brought on by an abundance of nervousness.

"Did we get the job done, or what? That should be your only concern. You don't ask for details, and we won't explain. Don't worry, I'll check in with my man. I promise, there'll be no more bodies involved, living or dead."

With that, the call was ended, and the man stepped into the bathroom. He splashed some water on his face and put his hair back in place. Satisfied that all trace of worry and concern had been erased, he opened the door and prepared for the coming of what and whomever may show.

***

"Bueno."

"The stakes are too high to keep pushing the envelope." The man laughed at what he thought was funny. "So, whatever you're doing at San Antonio's River Walk, if you're still doing it, and I don't want to know, I just need you to stop. Meanwhile, I'm depositing a little more dough into your account. Go get yourself some clothes so you can blend in with the crowd. You know, some shorts and a tank top or t-shirt. I don't know. For God's sake, it's over a hundred degrees in the shade there. You don't think an executive suit is gonna be noticed? What were you thinking?"

"Well, I *was* working, jefe."

The man was a hell of a hire, but not so well versed when it came to common sense.

"All I want you to do... Are you listening carefully? All I want you to do is continue to watch and see what happens. I never wanted you to do anything as drastic as kill someone, or two or three. That's a little overkill, don'tcha think?"

"Whatever you say, boss."

"Yeah, yeah, now go do some shopping. I expect to see a more appropriately attired surveillance selfie by tomorrow morning. Twenty-four hours. *Capiche*?"

Apparently he'd been watching too many Italian mafia movies. "Yeah sure. Whatever you say, boss."

***

Sometimes I could kick myself for leaving the blinds open just enough that it's the dawn's early light and not my alarm that awakens me. That's how I felt Tuesday morning. Sure, I had planned to open early enough to serve brunch to *las madres* who I hoped would choose Beta's to kick off their celebration, but at a quarter to seven, I still had hours of sleep calling to me.

Kacie must have sensed awakening life beneath the solitary sheet on my bed. She approached quietly, at least she would have if it hadn't been for the newly acquired collection of dog tags on her collar that announced her every twitch. Once the symphony neared my ears, she gave up all pretense of concern and fearlessly nosed her way into my hand and nudged me the rest of the way into existence.

"Good morning, girl. Did you come to wake your momma on this special day so we can rise and shine with a wonderful walk and a delicious non-kibble breakfast?" I'd spoken the W word. That did it. Kacie tugged and pulled, trying to get me out of bed. I rolled off the mattress, wiped the crusty sleepies from my eyes, and pulled on the shorts and tank top that hadn't made their way to the hamper after their last wearing. I'd wait to bathe until after we'd gone out to confront the already humid heat that awaited us.

The promise of a beautiful day greeted us, as we made our way around the 'hood. By the time we made it back home again, I couldn't wait to take the day full speed ahead. As soon as I opened the back door that led directly to the kitchen, I washed my hands, cracked some eggs, separated some bacon, and set both to fry in their designated pans. After putting some bread in the toaster, I opened the fridge. It wasn't too late to scramble them, but I chose to have them match my mood, sunny side up with a side of fresh melon. All the while, I was humming happily.

This was one of my favorite days. A day meant especially and exclusively for the celebration of women. There was nothing like being a mother. Although I, myself, had never given birth, for a while, I had been more of a mother to a child than her biological one had been. It's not necessary to endure the impregnation, gestation, labor, and delivery to bond with a baby. My heart swelled with the memory.

When we'd finished feasting and I'd finished washing the dishes, I gathered the goodies I'd be transporting for the occasion and looked at Kacie. "Are you coming with me? Or do you want to stay here?"

She tilted her head and looked at me as if she was considering.

"It's your choice, but it's gonna be a long day." I think it was the smells emanating from the dishes I was carrying that convinced her. She nearly bounced off the sofa to follow me.

Just as I unlocked the door to Beta's, I felt a presence.

"*Hola Tía, buenos días.*" Billie and Bety quickly approached me from behind with hugs and kisses. "*¡Feliz Día de la Tía!*"

I laughed. "That's right, *chicas*. Today we celebrate all mothers, aunts, cousins, neighbors, friends, whether they have children of their own or mother others, it makes no difference." Kacie joined them with a *woof* as if to say, *Aren't you forgetting someone?* "Thanks for the reminder, girl. And, of course, those fur moms who love and care for their fur babies." As if on cue, she wagged her tail and set off again in the direction of the kitchen, and we all laughed.

"Sorry we can't stay." Bety lamented. "We're still planning the day for Mom, who's kicking it off in her favorite way by sleeping in."

I laughed. "I envy her and hope your plans will include bringing her by, later today, at least for a few minutes."

"You know it," Billie said, "but only if you promise to save us some of your *riquísimos tamales*. And, of course, we'll be here later to help you out with serving."

"I've already set aside some in the fridge, and I can manage on my own if you decide to spend the whole day with your own mother. Now go on. Get out of here. *¡Ándale!*"

On their way out the door, they each stopped for their customary *besito* and left in their wake the sweet smell of fragrant perfume and vibrant youth. I immediately felt the intense profundity of the solitude surrounding me and hoped it was only temporary. Normally by this time, all tables at Beta's would be taken, and there would be a line of people waiting outside. Kacie sensed a sudden sadness in her human and whined briefly in compassionate solidarity.

"Oh come on, girl. We can't have you getting all teary and weepy, too." I walked behind the bar in search of some music in any genre but melancholy.

"*Éstas son las mañanitas.*" With my finger poised to hit the power button, the extremely off key singing of the wrong song for the holiday came from behind me. I turned to see Charlie and Di carrying chocolates, wine, and flowers my way.

"You, I understand, Charlie. But Di, surely you know it's not a birthday we're celebrating today."

"I beg to differ, and greatly. Many mothers are precisely that because they've given birth. Besides, we just wanted a cheerful way to get your attention. Now, stop being so *desagradecida*, these are for you. We can't let the darkness of these days rob us of all light and life."

"You got that right. Thank you so much." I smiled and took the gifts from them. "Have a seat. I'll be right back. I just want to get a vase, so I can get this beautiful bouquet in some water."

When I returned, I turned to Di. "So, what are your plans for the day?"

"I'm having a sale on anything even remotely related to mothers."

"And you, Charlie?"

"Well, I ordered some create-a-books for kids to give as presents to their mothers, and a number of fathers should be coming for them today. You know men, they wait until the last minute for everything." He laughed. "I'll try to talk as many as I can into hopping over here afterward."

"Why thank you, Charlie."

"And of course, I've had any and every book about mothers in my shop's front window for all to see, since the first of the month."

"Yes. I saw *Love You Forever*, the one with the little boy in the bathroom on the cover. It's such a beautiful story. All mothers should have a copy."

"Well, I've ordered plenty, so feel free to help me sell out."

"As much as I hate to be Debbie Downer and burst such a bright bubble with a prick of ugliness, we should devote at least a few minutes of the day to our feeble attempts at crime solving."

"You're right, of course, Bobbi. I just haven't thought of any more angles to explore. You, Di?"

She shook her head.

Business was so slow during lunch that I decided to do the unthinkable, something I'd never done. I closed for a few hours and went home. *On el mero día de las madres. Increíble.* I checked in with Di before leaving. She promised to give me a holler if she thought it'd be worth my while to come back sooner. If not, I'd reopen and see her at about five o'clock for what I hoped would be a dinner rush. Kacie and I took off. I felt like a kid skipping school. I'd later see this opportunity as a cause for distress, like when I'd sit to pay bills and find that my income fell far short of my outgo. For now, I decided to simply enjoy myself and some time off. Besides, I needed to do a little shopping.

***

"*Hola Trini, ¿cómo te ha ido?*" I greeted the owner of Las Flores de Trinidad, as I checked out her selection. Although I'd once been a frequent flier to her shop, those days and nights were long gone. Today's visit was for a different reason. My goal was to transform the image of my little waterfront area from the Night of the River Walking Dead horror story it had become. I wanted to celebrate *el día de las madres* in the most colorful and sweet-smelling way I knew how.

"*Bobbi, mi amor. ¿Cómo estás?* It's been a long time *mujer*." She came out from behind the buckets of bouquets to give me a kiss and a hug. "It's so good to see you."

"Same here, Trini. You know, work keeps me busy, or at least it did before the dawns of the dead."

"I can't believe it, Bobbi. And so close to you. I feel a little less afraid way over here, but not much, believe me." The bangles of her bracelets sang a sonorous song; Trini always talked with her hands.

"I hear you, Trini. Listen, I'm sorry to say I don't have all that much time to visit. I'm here for some blooms. What have you got?"

"Well, *mi amiga*, as you know, roses are always number one when it comes to love. Silky smooth petals...perfume... One can never go wrong." She batted her lashes and dialed up the flirt factor.

I laughed. "Hold on there, hot stuff. I'm not putting together a dozen for a lady love. I'm looking for some color to brighten my tables." I surveyed the buckets of freshly cut flowers. When she walked away to attend to another customer, I got an idea of what I wanted.

"Sorry about that *querida*. Have you found something you like?"

"Yes, as a matter of fact, I know exactly what I want. Can you put together about a dozen bunches of six flowers each, one for each color of the rainbow?"

"Ooooh. That will be so lovely. Just give me a few minutes to get them together. I think you'll be pleased with the results." Her flashing eyes revealed dilated pupils, and she hummed happily as she set out on her mission. Leaving her to the hunting, gathering, and beribboning, I took Kacie for a little walk. Without intent, we stumbled upon a pair of young lovers who'd apparently just discovered Love Lock Bridge. Lovers inscribe their initials on the locks, before attaching them to the bridge and tossing the keys into the San Antonio River. While the famous Parisian *Ponte des Artes* may have been removed, the local tradition appeared to be going strong. It made me happy and hopeful for those still hanging on, to the bridge and each other, to love.

By the time we returned, not more than a half hour later, Trini was excited to share the nosegays she'd put together. "I'm so happy, and I think you will be too," she excitedly exclaimed, before showing me the floral selection she'd artfully chosen. "To represent the color red, if you don't mind the little extra cost, I've placed a rose in the center of each bunch. I've surrounded it with some of the best wildflowers I have. The orange one is freesia. The yellow, of course, is a daisy. There's a bluebonnet, and for purple, I picked an aster. Instead of a flower for green, I thought the myrtle filler would do the job and offset the roses' cost. But, you tell me. What do *you* think?" She looked at me for an answer with hopeful anticipation. She'd already tied them in bunches, confident that I'd take them.

"They're perfect." I emphasized with a hug. And they were. I was happy with what she'd done in such a short time. There was definitely an art to the floral arrangement business. Trini set each bouquet in wet foam and nestled them all in a special cooler and sent me on my way with instructions to keep the truck's air conditioner running.

Wanting to keep the displays nice yet simple, I decided I'd put a few in some empty, colorful cans I had in the kitchen. I did splurge on a few *hecho-en-México* vases on my way home. I decided to leave Kacie on the couch, where she'd likely be most comfortable. Before heading back out, I snagged a few CDs for the day's special occasion. If Alejandra Guzmán singing *"Yo te esperaba"* didn't hit every Spanish-speaking mother in the feels, I didn't know what would.

***

Because my father had been a master sergeant in the United States Air Force, stationed at Lackland before his retirement, he had secured a plot for himself and my mother at Fort Sam Houston's National Cemetery. To this day, I felt an enormous sadness as I neared their simple, white-marble tombstone. *Raul Garza* was engraved on one side, and *Rebeca, loving wife and mother,* on the reverse. I cleaned the stone, placed the flowers, and sat on the ground to visit with my mother at her final resting place. I always brought music and memories. Today's choice was *"Algo se me fue contigo"* by Rocío Jurado.

I sat reverently and listened quietly, while the once-feisty Andalusian opened her heart and mine by way of her lyrical elegy. The same woman who had performed at the White House and Madison Square Garden, now sang for me, to my mother at her grave.

After the song had finished playing and I'd wiped the last of my tears away, I smiled at the memory of my mother's adulation of Jurado's feline eyes and reddish hair. Together we'd enjoyed and critiqued her many appearances. Years had passed since I'd thought of the romantic ballads that made the Spanish singer famous. I visited the memory of those precious moments spent with my mother, the love we'd shared. I could feel my mother's arms and love wrap tightly and warmly around me.

"Oh, Mami. No sabes cuánto te extraño." I stood and kissed the palm of my hand, before placing it on my mother's tombstone, then grave. "I love you," I whispered quietly, before grabbing my little boom box and wiping at more tears as I walked away.

Chapter Ten

AS SOON AS I got back to Beta's, I filled and placed the cans and vases strategically around the restaurant, hoping they would stand loud and proud until the night was done. I popped Guzmán's song in for a test run. Of course, just as the emotion in me flowed forth, Turner appeared. "Those damned *cebollas*," I explained the tears away. "I should have made Marcos cut them."

As I wiped my eyes on my shirt sleeve, she monitored my face before making direct eye contact and responding with a sad smile. Then finally seeing what else I was doing, she commented, "The flowers are beautiful."

"Thank you. A friend helped me with the arrangements. It's Mother's Day, at least for all the Mexicanas I'm hoping might spend some time with me."

She wrinkled her nose, cocked her head, and pursed her lips. "Wait. Mother's Day? Wasn't that last Sunday?"

"Here in the States, yes. In México, it's always celebrated on May 10, regardless of which day of the week the date falls on."

The corners of her eyes crinkled, as she watched me carefully cut the stems of the flowers to size. With a lopsided grin, she offered, "Do you need some help with those?"

"No, I'm almost done, but thanks anyway."

So far, no one had entered my pub in search of drinks or grub, so she and I took advantage of the time to talk.

"Are you here for business or pleasure?" Oh, if only I'd been able to capture the Kodak moment that flashed across her face. "I mean, are you working, or do you have the night off?" She wasn't in uniform, so what did I know? Maybe she'd stopped by to cash in on my previous offer.

She massaged between her eyebrows and lowered her head, before pressing her lips together with a pronounced sigh. "I'm afraid, until we catch the killer, I'm not likely to have any time for myself."

"Any news?" I Inquired.

She shook her head. "I'll be keeping an eye open here tonight, while some of the other blues will be combing the streets and parks, the general downtown area. We're hoping, if he plans to strike again, we can catch him before he does."

I didn't know what else to say. I was all out of small and business talk. After asking if I could provide her meal for the night, I excused myself and disappeared into the kitchen. At about the same time Marcos, Billie, and Bety showed up to save me from the day and myself.

Before I made it back out with her plate, a few people had taken seats at my tables. When I looked again, I realized it was the guys: Joseph, Danny, Paul, the whole bunch. They knew me so well. They'd come to cheer me up on a day that was notoriously difficult and painful for me.

***

Turner quietly observed Bobbi, who was busy behind the bar. A group came in and sat near her table. They were talking about the reasons why they had chosen this weeknight, in particular, to come to Bobbi's rescue.

"Poor Bobbi," Joseph lamented.

Turner's ears rotated like a satellite dish, tuning into the conversation. "I know you guys are her friends, but I'm not sure how well you know her."

"Well enough to know she could use some friends tonight," Danny shared. Dean and Robbie looked a little lost, so Danny explained. "Bobbi has *the* biggest heart. I love her, as everyone does, tons. She's always wanted to be a mother and was one for years. That's why this day is so hard on her." He reached for a chip.

"She was in a relationship with a woman," Joseph explained. "None of us liked her in the least. We knew she would someday break Bobbi's heart. I don't know all the details of its undoing, because Bobbi doesn't air any laundry, dirty or clean. She keeps it all hidden away and bottled tight. Anyway, the woman had a child who was pretty young at the time they got together. Bobbi was like another mother to the girl. It hit her hard when they broke up. Truth be known, I think it hurt her more to lose Rachel than it did to lose Lauren."

Shocked by what she'd heard and seeing how busy Bobbi had gotten, Turner decided she should go. She made eye contact with Bobbi, who was bringing a to-go container to her table.

"I'm gonna skedaddle and make this space available for a paying customer." Turner stood to leave.

"Wait!" Bobbi blurted out unexpectedly. "I want you to have some of these." She offered a small bouquet of flowers, then seemed to remember Turner was working. "They might be wilted and droopy by the time you finally get them home, but *'Si las flores pudieran' hablar...'*"

Paige's mother had flooded her daughter's memory with the sentimental songs of the Brazilian, Nelson Ned, but Paige hadn't revealed that she was practically bilingual. Bobbi would've had no idea that Paige caught the significance of those words.

She gave Bobbi a big smile. "Could you possibly keep them in a cool place for me, so they'll last? I'll come back for them before you leave. If that's okay?"

Bobbi smiled. She seemed to like the idea that they'd see each other again before the day ended. "Come whenever you're ready. These days and nights, I'd be foolish not to welcome customers, no matter how late. For you, my dear, I will gladly wait."

As Paige walked the river, she thought about all that she'd overheard Bobbi's friends say and compared the woman's love story to her own. Paige hadn't only inherited her mother's love of reading, but also her poor taste in life partners. She sucked at relationships but she clung to the hope that her luck would change. Her mother's had. Paige's problem, she knew, stemmed from a subconscious desire to protect and serve victims of abuse, women like her mother, from the hands and weapons that threatened and controlled them. Although such an innately developed desire had been a major force in her career choice, ironically, it hadn't served to protect her from partnering romantically with women who used and abused her. Not that any of them had ever done so in a physical way.

She always seemed to find herself drawn toward women who needed to be taken care of but who failed to love her in the way that she wanted and craved. She accepted full responsibility and acknowledged the role she'd always seemed to willingly play. She hoped and was holding out for a true partnership of equals, a reciprocal, romantic, emotional and physical give and take. Her thoughts again turned Bobbi's way and to the flowers. She smiled a moment, then cleared her mind in order to return her full attention to hunting a killer. What a welcome she'd received to San Antonio.

***

The mothers had cleared out long before closing time, to continue celebrating at home with their families. I smiled at the memories I had of times with Rachel, once upon a seemingly long time ago, and sent my *sobrinas* home to spend some more time with their own mother.

"Take these home to your mother, and tell her I'll call her in the morning." I loaded their arms with plates and bowls of fajita meat, beans, and rice. "It's a little heavy for this late at night, but who says you can only celebrate mothers on one day?" I kissed them both goodbye. "*Hasta pronto, chicas.*"

"Bye Tía. Love you."

Since I'd told Turner I'd wait for her to return, I sat with my computer and opened the mail. I wrote checks to cover the most important bills, some overdue. I paid rent, water, electric, and food suppliers, then did a quick run through of the rest of the pile. *Mostly junk, no surprise.* I stopped when I came upon what looked like a more personal piece of correspondence. The name of the business was handwritten on the front.

I opened it to find an offer for Beta's. Obviously the sender wrongly assumed the owner of this property ran the place. Even though it wasn't for me, since I'd already opened it, I decided to see how much the prospective buyer was willing to pay. My mouth almost hit the floor at the sight of the figures before my wide eyes. Such was the expression on my face when Turner reappeared. She had such impeccable timing.

"What's that you've got there? Judging by the look on your face, I'm guessing it could be anything from an eviction notice to notification that you've just inherited multimillions from some unknown relative." She looked at me a little sideways.

I laughed. "I hope you're not gonna bust me for opening someone else's mail. This little beauty is definitely not for me."

"What is it? Can I see?"

"Sure, that way you'll have committed as much of a federal offense as me." I handed it over.

"Guilty as charged." She gave the paper a quick read. "That sure seems like a tempting offer. Someone must be extremely interested in this place."

I nodded.

"What are you going to do with it?"

"Well, seeing as how I recently renewed a three-year lease, I guess it could be a win-win for me, either way." She looked perplexed by my statement, and I opened my arms to encompass the still-to-be-paid bills that lay on the table before me. "It's no secret that business was already floundering. Now...well, I fear more people will be staying away. Maybe it'll prove to be a blessing in disguise for me. A way out without having to break the lease. The owner will win either way, with this kind of interest in the property."

Turner nodded. "It's sad to see small businesses go under. The big businesses are always so much less personable. It's a shame."

"Well, I'm not throwing my towel in yet." I emphasized my dogged determination by tugging on the terrycloth dish towel and table wiper I wore as a permanent accessory. "So, how'd your evening go? Any insights tonight?"

"None." She sighed, obviously frustrated. "Now, about those flowers."

"Oh jeez. I almost forgot." I turned and headed for the kitchen. When I returned, I handed them to her for the second time that night. "I apologize for the chill. I thought they might last a little longer if I put them in the fridge."

Turner maintained eye contact, while lowering her head. She smiled sheepishly before sticking her nose into the bunch. "They're nice, Bobbi. They smell so pretty. I don't remember the last time someone gave me flowers. Thank you."

Was it my imagination? Or did her eyelashes flutter slightly?

There was nothing, absolutely nothing, I could do to control the deep red of the blush that flushed over my face from the bottom of my neck to my graying hairline.

"By the way, you didn't really steal these, did you?" She gestured with the flowers.

I touched the base of my neck, pulled my brows together and chewed my lip. *Why would she ask me that?* The look on my face, I suspected, was similar to what she'd seen when she first came inside.

"'*Si las flores pudieran' hablar...* If I'm not mistaken, that's the title of a romantically sentimental Nelson Ned song." She paused there, no doubt to prolong my torturous agony. "I remember that some of the other lyrics explain where those flowers came from. And well, since I *am* a law enforcement officer, there's *that* little matter. And because I am also a woman, I'm just wondering how many of the words of that song you were hoping the flowers would say to me."

I covered my heart with my hand. Yes, I was emoting. "*Ay mi corazóncito y Dios mío.* I had no idea you speak Spanish."

Turner laughed. "I'm so sorry I didn't tell you sooner. I would have, but it's been kinda cute and fun listening and learning a few things I'm sure you would have never spoken in front of, much less to me had you known."

Oh my God! What had I revealed?

"Don't worry," she responded as if reading my mind and answering my unasked question. "You didn't say anything *overly* embarrassing." There was that smile again. "Someday, when this is all over with, maybe we'll find some time to talk about more than dead bodies and the grime of crime, and get to know each other on a much more pleasant and personal level."

All I could do was stand there with my mouth hanging open.

"For now, since I'm here, how about I walk with you to your car?"

I gathered my things, closed my mouth, wiped my drool, and for some reason felt the need to set her straight. "My truck. I have a truck."

"Of course you do." She smiled.

Should I be offended? Did she now see me as the epitome of a diesel dyke? A stereotype?

Before I mustered the courage to ask, she filled the ensuing silence, "Most everyone in Texas does."

We walked in companionable silence, until we reached the end of the block. I hoped and prayed she wouldn't realize we were circling to the rear of my place. We could have simply walked through my restaurant and out the back door.

"Well, this is me. Thank you for walking me to my old jalopy with the manual windows." As I turned to put the key in the door, I shared a nagging thought. "Do you think it's possible that the prospective buyer would kill to get what he or she wants?"

She cocked her head, raised her eyebrows, and partially opened her lips. *Was she preparing for a kiss?* Ha. I could only wish. No, it was much more likely a prelude to the clenched jaw, red face, curled lip, and pulsing neck veins.

I begged of her, "Just hear me out. This is not the first time I've received such an offer."

The rigid expression that appeared on her face erased all that remained of my fantasy. "And you didn't think to tell me this before, because—"

"I didn't think it meant anything, but now..."

She pressed her lips together in a tight line before demanding, "Go on."

I cringed at the thought of telling her what was coming next. "I'm not the only one who's received them. Diane, Charlie, I think even Delgado. Maybe others, I don't know."

She shook her head and frowned at me. "I need to look at that letter again. Can I stop by in the morning?"

"I can save you the trouble. I'm pretty sure I have at least one in my truck."

"At least one. How many have you received? How long has this been going on?"

Chapter Eleven

THE MAN SHUFFLED ALONG, searching. He passed a few moored barges and a number of restaurants. If any of them were what he was seeking, no one would have guessed by the way he behaved. He continued walking, as if trying to get a feel for the place. The river was nearly deserted. It was late. There was no reason for him, or anyone else, to be there, unless they were looking for trouble. That's how targets were made, how trouble received an invitation to come your way. The man had read about individuals who had been found drowned in the water, whether by accident, intent, or foul play, even before the most recent floater made the newspaper's front page. He knew there had also been a few stabbings, some gunshot wounds, and fights that broke out after brawlers spilled out of nearby bars in search of other outlets for their anger and frustrations. All such humans were highly volatile. Not all were intoxicated.

He stopped a while, as if to study one particular stretch along the waterway. Seemingly satisfied with his find, he turned abruptly and walked back in the direction from whence he'd come. He walked with purpose, as if a decision had been made.

Deep within a tunnel that ran under Highway 281, amidst sofas spilling their stuffing and chairs stained with God only knew what, the man stepped over hypodermic needles, broken glass, and the stench of rodent-enticing trash. He scouted carefully for the next sacrificial lamb.

When news of Seguin Park's connection to the killings was splashed all over the front page of the city's only newspaper, the man had lost precious time seeking out a different venue for his purposes. An online search of the paper's archives revealed a story about the discovery of a massive underground tunnel, where dozens, if not hundreds, of homeless were living. Although the inhabitants of that encampment had since been removed and relocated, there were bound to be many more just like it. There was no way the city had the resources to do more than occasional cleanups of these places.

It didn't take him long to find one, and he didn't have to go all that far in his search. After all, it made sense that the homeless would try to stay close to what few resources they had at their disposal, the soup kitchens and public libraries, food, air-conditioning, a restroom, and entertainment.

He'd become a pro at singling out those who proved to be most receptive to his promises of easy money. A creature of habit, tonight he had a particular prey in mind. Once he'd settled on his mark, he closed in on the young man, made a little small talk, and dangled what must have been a 14K gold carrot in the youth's face. *One man's junk is another man's treasure.* Unbeknownst to the about-to-be hired actor, the one-act performance he bargained for would be his final staged play.

***

Just what is it about the woman? Paige found herself thinking of Bobbi on the way home that evening. She was so unlike any of the others Paige had dated. For starters, they hadn't met at a bar. Well actually, they had, but not in *that* way, nor on some dating website. The attraction she felt to Bobbi was developing slowly rather than being forced or blinded by the alcohol content of a few drinks. That was a new, definitely different, good thing. She closed her eyes and envisioned the woman's mischievously sparkling, brown eyes with such soulful expressiveness. Paige sighed wistfully. Unfortunately, she'd have to turn the heat of that burner to simmer until this crime was solved, then maybe she could have some semblance of a personal life again.

She was feeling bad for having left Bobbi as abruptly as she did, but once she had the offer in her hand, she couldn't wait to get home and research the wannabe buyer. She had to see if she could find any link to the murders.

She let Kona out to potty. While she waited, she re-read the pages of the offer.

From what she could tell, CBI Partners of Houston had been shopping real estate to a myriad of well-financed developers. Apparently, they made their money by sending out offers like these and bundling multiple properties together for a sizable and more attractive development opportunity. She thought about Beta's, The Blue Burro, and Rainbow Reads. At first, she couldn't imagine anyone being interested enough to kill to have those small businesses. When she considered their combined square footage, however, she realized there was plenty of space that had the added incentive of being within walking distance of the Tobin Center for the Performing Arts. *Why didn't I think of this? How can I find out which investors might be interested?*

With these kinds of promising new leads, she'd never get any sleep.

She looked at the flowers Bobbi had given her. She smiled, despite an overwhelming sense of sadness she'd begun feeling. She missed the mother who'd instilled in her so many loving and wonderful memories, who'd worked so hard and sacrificed so much to raise her. She missed her immensely.

Paige thought about how, when she was young, they would walk together, hand in hand, to the downtown public library and spend hours browsing books in the collection. She smiled at the memory of a particularly cold day when sounds were amplified by cloud cover and their breath could be seen in the air.

"Can you hear them?" her mother asked.

Paige nodded enthusiastically with an unbridled child's imagination.

"What do you hear?" her mother tested her.

"The hooves," Paige responded.

There were no horses, but they were walking a Dickensian cobblestone street. Like mother, like daughter. The gift of creative vision had been passed on.

Later, when her mother was on the three to eleven shift at the college library, ten-year-old Paige would often accompany her and never dream of complaining. It was an adventure. Although she'd always loved to read, it was there, amidst the four floors filled with stacks of books, that she'd developed a love for the used and abused, the abandoned tomes left open in chairs, piled in study carrels, or haphazardly strewn over tables. She loved pushing the media cart up and down the aisles and collecting the books, while her mother worked at the circulation desk. Along the way, a young Paige pushed in chairs and lowered blinds to a uniform level within all the windows' casings, giving the library a pleasing and cared-for appearance.

She didn't remember much about her father and thought that was for the best. Other than a few painful pictures in her mind, all she remembered was eavesdropping on adult conversations in hushed tones after their separation. Sometimes, you should judge a book by its cover, especially when it hints at a story of horror and terror. She shivered at one of the few memories she retained of a physical altercation, when she'd crawled under her bed and cried beneath the metal springs. Paige wasn't sure why she had even kept the man's last name.

As an adult, and especially one in her profession, she realized her mother should have had her father put behind bars. It broke her heart when she later learned what her mother had endured in an attempt to keep her family together for her daughter's sake. Paige gave thanks to God for the man her mother later met and married. He had been a good husband and father figure.

***

While still slightly embarrassed by the awareness that Turner had been privy to my private longings all along, I was even more dismayed when she swiftly took leave of my company. After feeding Kacie, I sat with my thoughts of her, on the couch in front of a TV I wasn't watching. I wasn't sure how much faith I put into the theory I'd proposed. Was it a plausible motive for murder? We desperately needed to identify the killer, so we could find him and lock him away. *We.* I liked the sound of the word and all that its two little letters implied. I reached for the remote and clicked on the television. Imagine that, ID TV opened on the screen.

***

"Tell me, please, why am *I* now getting an offer for *my* place? Have you forgotten who's paying you to deliver these?"

The faceless bastard gave a sardonic laugh. "Surely, you must realize you're not the only man I work for, Señor Delgado."

Delgado pushed the button to disconnect the call, wishing he could so easily sever his connection to the man at the other end of the line. Unfortunately, these were not the type of people one could disengage from easily. In all likelihood, the anonymous voice, whether he liked it or not, was destined to be on his payroll for life.

He looked at the offer made for his restaurant. He had no intention of selling the place. As a matter of fact, his interest was in buying the other properties. Those owners should have received similar letters he'd written himself. Although...he looked again to be sure. His offers had much smaller numbers on the buy line. *What the hell is going on here?*

For years, he'd hoped to be able to buy those paltry little plots of land on the other side of the river and expand his business. He'd intentionally kept seafood off La China Poblana's menu, only offering it from time to time to test its marketability. Now that he was at a place where he could venture forth with his intention, all he needed was a site for the restaurant he was already calling La Veracruzana. He planned to have an entrance both off the downtown street at the rear of the restaurant and on the lower level on the river. He'd need all three properties to make his culinary dream come true. He was practicing patience, but ready to pounce. After all, it would take a while to get it built and ready for a grand opening. That's why he had resorted to hiring a mystery middleman, who was apparently two-timing. He wondered what this other dealmaker had in mind.

***

Terry Bigelow owned several lucrative gambling establishments, ranging from small and smoky poker rooms to the slots and table games of high roller casinos. He reached for his ringing phone.

"Bigelow."

"Hey boss. Just wanna let you know that Delgado's asking questions."

Bigelow laughed. "So, I take it that he finally got around to opening his mail. Well, let him sit on it for a while. I'm not ready to raise the ante just yet. Although, I can't afford to let him outbid me and walk away with even one of the properties. I need them all, plus some, to turn my dream into a reality. For now, just do what you've been doing. Keep an eye on him, on all of them. If they don't bite soon, we'll move to phase two." With that, Bigelow cut the call.

The ambitious man walked to the wall that displayed his future San Antonio River Walk casino. Texas gamblers had been clamoring for it for years. He was pretty confident that, with enough cold, hard cash in hand, he could swing opinion and votes in his favor. If push came to shove, he'd find another way. Why let all that hard-earned oil money leave the state to the table games of Oklahoma and Louisiana? Worse yet, Vegas. He'd seen the stats and knew how much was squandered away in Sin City.

He rubbed his hands together in greed, salivating around the end of his Cuban cigar.

***

A day passed without a dead body in the vicinity. The river and its surrounding parks and downtown streets seemed to be relatively safe, at least as safe as they'd been before the killings. There was always the possibility that lost time would be made up for with multiple killings on a future day. In his uncertainty, Flynn didn't know where to turn for crime stories that could possibly sell as many newspapers as San Antonio's River Walk murders. They'd been on a roll, and he'd been in his glory. Now, the city was back to same old, same old. Suddenly, a light bulb exploded in his head, with a powerful surge of electricity.

He jumped out of his chair so fast, he left it spinning behind him. He grabbed his messenger bag, threw the strap over his shoulder, and raced out of the building. Night was falling. There was no time to waste.

***

He escorted the young man out of the tunnel without revealing he'd already ingested a potentially lethal overdose. He saw a familiar face headed their way. Before they could be seen, he pulled the young man back inside to wait.

"You know where to go, right?"

The young man indicated that he did.

"Go on ahead. I'll be there soon. The pill I gave you will help you lay still, but it will wear off before sunrise when your job is done. I'll give you the rest of your money at that time."

The young actor took off in the direction of the river, while the director remained in the shadows.

Sneaking a peek out from the darkness, the man watched. *Why is he here?* Out of sight, the man listened as Flynn questioned the others. *He's going to get himself killed if he isn't careful.* He waited for Flynn to disappear into the depths of the concrete jungle, before seizing his chance to slide away, unseen.

The director would have liked to observe his theatrical production, but he knew it was a risk he couldn't take. The river was being watched. It was not a safe place for him to be, especially at this time of night. He'd have to settle for reading about his efforts in the newspaper, assuming the boy's body would be discovered before the deadline. Too wired to sleep, he walked to his nearby office building. It helped, immensely, that he had the type of job that almost expected one to work all and odd hours.

***

Back at his desk, the journalist settled comfortably in his chair, both energized and inspired. The words flowed freely from his mind through his body and out his fingertips. He plugged his earbud in and cranked Daughtry's "Bring Me to Life." The keyboard could barely keep pace with the tempo of his typing.

Chapter Twelve

UNABLE TO SLEEP, I grew tired of tossing and turning and decided to get an early start to the day. It was still dark out. For normal people, it was still, practically, the middle of the night. *What the hell, it'll give me time to tinker around in the kitchen and maybe concoct a new menu item.*

"C'mon Kacie. You can keep me company in the predawn twilight."

The dog happily accepted my invitation.

The streets were empty. Most everyone with any ounce of sanity was still asleep. I envied such people. I pulled into my usual space behind the cantina and unlocked the back door. While I'd often stayed late, well into the dark of night, I'd never been in so early. It was eerie. I turned the lights on in an effort to chase out any overnight, human squatters that might have found a way into my sacrosanct space or just phantasmic products of my overactive imagination.

Since not a creature stirred, I rooted through my cabinets in search of inspiration. I didn't get far before noticing Kacie was acting strangely. Where she most always was so quiet and settled, she couldn't seem to get comfortable. Instead, she kept circling and pacing. *What on earth?* "*¿Qué te pasa chica?*"

Against my better judgment, I snapped on her leash and took her out the front door, hoping a little walk would help calm her and ease my own anxiety. When we returned, I'd fix us both some breakfast. Maybe my getting out of bed at such an unusual hour had caused her to think it was time to eat. *¿Tienes hambre?*

We hadn't gone far, when Kacie kicked her uncommon behavior up a notch, just as we were walking past one of the river barges' boarding docks. A floating vessel had either been left moored overnight or was already awaiting its first morning arrivals. I let out her leash and allowed her to follow her nose to whatever had her so excited. As she took us closer to the boat, I could see there was something on the floor between the rows of inward facing seats. *¡Sálvame Señor! Is that a …? Could it be un muerto?*

I couldn't believe I didn't have Turner's number on speed dial, or for that matter, at all. *What kind of poor excuse for a stalker was I?* I moved cautiously, quietly, and ever so slowly closer to the dark lump curled on the dory's flat bottom. Daring a glance over its sides, I soon realized there was, indeed, a man there. Not yet a corpse, but a still living and breathing being. I pulled out my phone and hit 9-1-1, all the while looking around for anyone who might be waiting to finish off the job.

I praised Kacie, "Good girl. You did good bringing me here this morning." She wagged her tail and licked my face. I had no fear with her by my side, while I waited for help to arrive.

Suddenly and unexpectedly, the man stirred and attempted to rise. What else could I do? I went to him, hoping this wasn't the killer's modus operandi. As protective weaponry goes, so not the girly type, I wasn't even packing a nail file. Admittedly putting my life on the line, I stepped into the boat and closed the gap between us with each size-six footstep of mine.

"Hello," I whispered into the night. "Can you hear me?"

His movement stopped and he made some kind of noise with his mouth, I leaned in to better hear him above the din of my heart's pounding.

"Is that you?"

"Who are you looking for?" I wanted to know.

Ignoring my question, he flailed against the rail of what could have been his floating coffin if I hadn't happened by.

"You didn't tell me I was going to feel this bad. What did you give me, anyway?"

I lowered the timbre of my voice and channeled my inner masculinity, assuming it had been a male who orchestrated the scene that was unfolding before my eyes. "*No te preocupes.* You'll be fine. Now, just so I can know you're with it enough to remember, what was it I told you to do? What was your mission tonight?"

"You told me to go to the river and slip into this barge."

"That's not all. *¿Qué más?*" I chanced.

"You told me to wait here until I was discovered, until I scared someone. You told me, by sunrise, the drug you gave me to help me lay still through the night would be out of my system."

At this point in our conversation, the man still hadn't faced me. He'd been lying on his stomach the whole time. I guess the drug had depressed his body; he was slurring his words slightly. I could only hope he was lucid enough to be telling me the truth and about to paint me a reliable picture of the man I was looking for.

"Do you remember what I look like?"

I had to ask the question twice.

"Why would you ask me that?"

"Just testing your memory to make sure the drug is wearing off like it should."

I committed the information he gave me to memory just before the emergency crew and officers in blue arrived.

***

"What do you mean I'm a suspect?" I responded incredulously.

"Well, you *were* the last person to see the man alive."

"And, I was also the person who tried to save his life by calling *you*. He was alive when *you* got here," I corrected the officer. *Where the hell is Turner when I need her?* "If I had done anything to harm him, do you think I'd be dumb enough to incriminate myself by getting involved?"

Okay, I need to check myself before it's too late.

"So, what does that mean? What do you want from me? I've told you everything."

Actually, I hadn't, but he didn't need to know that. I sure wasn't gonna tell him.

I must admit, I was surprised that the young man had died. I mean, I'd just been talking to him when—*Bam!*— All of a sudden, he was gone.

***

Although she'd begun to look forward to volunteer shifts at St. Benedict's, Paige had requested the community service coordinators give her a different venue, claiming she needed a change of pace. What she wanted was a chance to get out and about, to mingle freely and unsuspiciously with the unserved and underserved, the people most desperately in need. While word had gotten around about the free eats, they didn't all know about the many available opportunities of which they could partake.

She approached her first victim—*Given the circumstances, maybe I should think of the woman in a different way*—and offered her a cheerful greeting, "Good morning." The woman looked at her and smiled, making it easier to feel like she wasn't invading and entirely unwelcome. She didn't know how salespeople did it. "My name is Paige, and I'm with St. Benedict's, here to share with you about our ministry."

"Ministry?" The woman appeared to immediately go on the defensive and physically backed away a little. "I ain't interested in no church or religion. God ain't got no good for a wretch like me." She looked at Paige appraisingly. "What are you, anyway? Mormon? They seem to be everywhere these days. Moving in from Utah. I wouldn't mind so much if it had been Donny and Marie back in the day." The woman smiled at her own funny, but not in a mean way. The woman's choice of words led Paige to believe she was not completely ignorant of the Bible or its teachings.

"Oh, not that kind of ministry. We're just out spreading the word, making sure you all know you have a place to go when you're cold or hungry."

The woman laughed out loud. "How 'bout when I'm hot in this miserable-ass hundred degree heat? You got a pool I can swim in or lounge beside with a nice cool umbrella drink?"

Paige couldn't help but smile at the woman's good-natured spirit. She was liking her already.

"Never mind. I already got a place to go when I reach my maximum level of endurance, no thanks to the South Texas heat." She looked at Paige, as if wondering if she should share her secret. "The Big Red Enchilada on Soledad Street. You know where I mean?" Paige hadn't been in town long enough to learn all of the locals' special terms for places. This was a new one for her, so she shrugged, raised her brows, and twisted her mouth into a lopsided grin. She didn't have a clue what the woman was talking about. "The library, honey. Are you new in town?"

Paige nodded.

"It helps that I like to read. They got some nice comfy chairs there. I don't have an address or driver's license so I can't get a card or use their technology, but their bathrooms help me stay a little clean." She glanced away and held her chin close to her body before continuing, "There's a real nice lady works there. Her name's Calliope Jayne, least that's what she told me. She keeps my books behind the desk for me, so no one can check them out while I'm in the middle of reading them, and she hides a little bottle of perfume behind a certain toilet for me."

Paige got the impression this woman could talk for days, and while she loved learning and listening, she had business to take care of and didn't have time to talk. She cut to the chase. "Do you mind if I ask your name?"

"Dorothy. My name's Dorothy, but I like you." She smiled. "So you can call me Dottie."

"Well, thank you, Dottie. I'm pleased to meet you. And, as much as I'd like nothing better than to sit and chat with you all day, I'm afraid I am working, or supposed to be." She smiled at her new friend. "Let me leave you with these brochures. They tell all about our services, and you told me you like to read."

Paige prepared to move on to the next willing listener but decided to commingle her jobs. She turned back to Dottie. "Before I go, if you don't mind, I have a few questions I'd like to ask."

"Go for it, honey. I'm listening."

Paige smiled again.

"I just want to make sure you feel safe here, well, as safe as you can."

With a gentle smile that reached her eyes, the woman expressed her gratitude, "Thanks for caring about me, but as you can see, my house ain't got no front door to lock. But, I ain't exactly got nothing nobody'd want anyway, so I reckon I'll be okay."

Paige didn't want to scare the woman and rob her of any remaining peace, but she felt like she should make sure she was aware of the dangers of living on the street, especially these days.

As if Dottie could read her mind, she assured her, "Honey, don't you worry none about me. I've been living on the streets for a long time now. I know how to take care of myself." As if to prove her point, she shared, "I sleep with one eye open, keep a bottle I can break if needed at an arm's reach, and I can smell trouble coming from a mile away, despite all the nasty aromas that surround me."

Paige breathed a little easier. "I'm happy to know that, Dottie. Tell me, have you seen anyone around lately who looks like they might be looking for something or someone? Someone who might be studying the place? Or—"

"Are you asking me if maybe I've seen whoever it is that's trying to rid San Antonio of its homeless population?" In response to Paige's raised and curved brows, Dottie shared, "Yes, I know. Remember, I like to read. And the library still carries the local newspaper for vagabonds like me." She smiled softly, merely acknowledging her current lot in life, not self-deprecating. "Unfortunately for you, but fortunately for me, I can't say I've seen anyone I'd suspect was someone looking to kill me."

"Well, do me a favor, will you? If you happen to see, or hear, of anyone that you think might be a threat or pose any danger, promise me you'll let me or one of the other volunteers or police officers who show on your doorstep know, as soon as you're able."

Dottie stared at her with half-lidded eyes. With pursed lips and an index finger pressed to her cheek, Dottie propped her chin on the rest of her clenched fingers before speaking.

"What if the killer is pretending to be or is, one of us?" She got Paige thinking about a possibility she hadn't considered.

***

Homicide detectives are investigating, after a man's body was found early Wednesday morning in a river barge moored at the Dolorosa dock, making it the fifth body to appear on the San Antonio River Walk since Thursday. Local merchant, Roberta Garza, found the body while out walking her dog. Investigators are securing surveillance footage from cameras in the area and ask anyone with any information to please call their Crime Solvers hotline at 555-0100.

I'd barely set the paper on the bar, when Turner walked in, not looking all that happy with me.

"I had to find out from the morning paper that it was *you* who found the body?"

With just one semiloud accusation, I decided I was liking this side of my babe in blue. *I bet she could be some kinda fiery hot.* She already was, in my imagination.

I shrugged. "You've never given me your number."

"Give me your phone," she demanded.

I handed it over immediately. While I pondered the possibility of other forceful commands she might someday, or night, whip my way in more pleasurable play, she added herself as a contact before handing the phone back to me.

I had no intention to tell her what I'd discovered, but she was looking an unfun kind of angry, so I walked to a table and pulled a chair out, indicating she should take a seat.

"*Por favor, no te enojes.*"

"Oh. So there's more?"

I nodded shyly, as I worked hard to push the words out. She seemed to be losing patience, so I thrust them over my tongue. I didn't think it was a good time to keep her waiting. "The dead man kinda spoke a few words to me before your buddies in blue arrived."

She sat back and glared at me. I couldn't tell if she was getting madder, intrigued, or feeling some other way emotionally. Without any verbal prompting on her part, I told her everything. "*No sabía qué hacer.* I wanted to tell you, but you weren't there, and I didn't know how to find you."

She must have been thinking and calculating the whole time I was talking, because she clicked on her phone and checked the time before stating, "We now have less than twenty-four hours to figure this out and stop him before he takes another life."

Of course, the mention of twenty-four hours made me think of Kiefer Sutherland's character, but I didn't think this was the best time to share the fantasy I harbored of her as my own, female, Jack Bauer.

"Let's go over this again," she suggested. "All we know is that he came from a tunnel encampment, and he walked here. So, it can't be too far. I guess the first thing we need to do is figure out which one."

A sudden thought screamed to be let out of my mind. "What if there's a pattern that we've been missing?"

She looked at me, listening, and waiting for me to go on.

"First, there was the *hombre en el río.* Then, the woman *en la tortilla.* Then, *la pareja,* a man and a woman. And, now *este hombre.* I think I read somewhere that serial killers, and that's what this is, right? often kill in patterns of some sort. What if, for whatever reason, he's moving from male to female and cycling genders. That would mean his next target will be a homeless woman."

As soon as the words were out of my mouth, I could tell that my serve-and-protect hero was seriously considering going deep under dirty cover. There was absolutely no way the best makeup artist from Hollywood could help her pull off a disguise as a homeless woman. While I, on the other hand … On second thought, no one would ever believe a chunky monkey like me was on the soup-kitchen diet. I guess we'd have to do our best with Turner and pray for poor lighting.

Chapter Thirteen

"HOW'S THAT?"

"I wouldn't touch you with a ten-foot pole, but, you're still gonna need to add a little funk to your trunk to be convincing."

"Do you truly think he's going to be sniffing around for authenticity?"

I shrugged. "Just go outside in the hot sun for a while, and if you have deodorant on, wash it off. God, did you *have* to wash your hair this morning?"

"Well, I'm *sorry*. I didn't realize there'd be a need to sacrifice my hygiene on such short notice."

We bantered back and forth like that for more than an hour, battling the anxiety that wrapped tightly around both of us. I'd taken Turner to my place, where I could get my hands on her, and on some backyard dirt, and where I had the right instruments to tease her hair into a beautiful mess of twisted and matted locks of less than loveliness. I sent forth a silent prayer that she'd forgive her impromptu cosmetologist if the damage proved to be permanent. I sent out another for the poor people who had to live in such conditions daily. I scuffed up and tore some of my old clothes that I knew would be big on her. Pristine, hip-hugging, titty-tugging garments wouldn't do for this occasion.

As I worked on her, she looked around the little, seven-hundred-square-foot, Tobin Hill place I called home, the entirety of which could be seen from where we were, save for the bedroom. My throat constricted a little on that thought, and I put a choke hold on my mental wanderings.

"I like your place," she shared. "It feels so warm and homey."

"*Gracias*. It's good enough for me."

She looked at me with an expression that couldn't be deciphered. I interpreted it as a longing of sorts, although I couldn't imagine what I could possibly have that she'd want. While my little apartment was comfy and cozy to me, it was more like Motel 6 than the Ritz. Okay, maybe I was selling my place a little short. There's no place like home. I think most everyone who has one feels the same way.

"That should do it." I spun her around for a 360-degree look.

She stood and walked to the bathroom, so she could see for herself.

"Now, don't carry yourself so well. Slouch a little. No matter where you've come from, a couple of nights on concrete will take the pep out of anyone's step. There, that's better." I voiced my approval as she slowed her roll. As if I knew what the hell I was talking about.

* * *

As unhappy as she was about it, we'd decided to divide and conquer. Time was of the essence and the clock, like a bomb set to go off, was loudly ticking. It was my turn for a makeunder. After considering the puny assortment of options available, I opted for a dress I didn't even know I had, hidden deep in the back of my closet.

"What's that?" I teased after hearing an attempt to suppress a giggle at the sight of me.

"When was the last time you wore this?" Turner asked. She lifted the gauzy fabric, prompting me to give a little twirl and bat my nearly nonexistent lashes like some femme fatale. Surely there was some irony to be found in that expression, but not now.

I looked at my watch and realized we needed to get to business. Time to prepare ourselves in other than physical ways.

When we were both ready, we hopped in my truck and headed out. I dropped her two blocks from where she'd be headed and prepared to drive on to my first designated port of entry. We'd already mapped out where I'd leave our ride, and how and when we'd meet again.

"You have my number, right?" Turner wanted to be sure before I took off.

"Right here next to my heart." I patted the left cup of my padded bra.

"And yours is in my pocket." She ran her hand along her upper thigh, stopping only after she'd felt it.

"You mean that's not a rocket?" I had to joke to break the tension. My efforts got me a sly smile. "*Ten cuidado,*" I called to her as she walked away.

She turned and pleaded, with a look of genuine concern that nearly melted all of me.

"You, too,"

***

Maybe it was beginner's luck. Maybe I just happened to be in the right place at the right time. Whatever, the man approached me while I was rummaging through an old, rusty shopping cart. I hoped the owner of the possessions inside wouldn't show up right now.

"Hello there."

I momentarily froze, as I heard the unexpected greeting from somewhere behind me. I had my back to him and was almost afraid of what I'd find when I turned around to face him. When I mustered the nerve, I saw the man was nothing like I'd expected, given Barge Boy's description and my imagination. Even if he'd shaved and attempted a different hairpiece, there was no way this was the mystery man we'd all seen out of disguise. *Guess I lost that bet.* This guy had a good six inches on the other, and his skin color was about three shades lighter than I remembered. In character, I eyed him suspiciously without responding.

"Are you looking for something special? Maybe something I can help you find?" Without taking his eyes off mine, his fingers shook a small, transparent bag he held in his right hand. I looked at the powdery white substance he offered, before looking again at his eyes, so he'd know I'd seen his offering.

I summoned every theatrical god and goddess I could think of to help me pull off this charade. I stepped down from the rung on the cart and hoped I'd managed to express an interest by way of the look in my eyes.

"All I need you to do," he attempted to seduce me with both his wares and his words, "is to put on a little show for me."

I looked at him, begging for understanding.

"You see, I'm trying to scare some people by making them think there's a dead body on the river."

The coldest of arctic shivers chilled my icy spine. This was it, he was him. This was the real deal. *How am I going to make it out of this alive?* Finally, I spoke. "But there have been *muertos* on the river." I couldn't help it. I just blurted out the cold, hard truth.

His mouth stretched in a demonic smile. "You're not going to be one of them. All you have to do is pretend to be dead until you're discovered and your body's finder runs away in fear. After that, you can simply walk away."

Yeah, I bet that's what you told the last guy. The only place he walked away to was his grave.

"I'll tell you where to wait and front you a little taste of this." He shook the plastic bag. "Take it before you settle in place, to help keep you calm and still while you wait."

I took the bag from his hand and awaited further instruction. He seemed to be thinking aloud, as if he hadn't decided yet, "I want it to be someplace everyone who has walked *el Paseo del Río* will recognize." Suddenly, it appeared inspiration lit his face from within. "I know the perfect place." He pulled out his phone and showed me a picture of two well-known destinations. "Either of these will be fine. They are both places everyone stops for photo ops. I'll let you choose." He showed me the Staircase Falls, and one of the weathered stairways with decorative tiles. I happened to know that most tourists make a stop at the place where water cascades over descending cement landings.

"I know where this is," I told him as I pointed to my chosen place.

"Good," he exclaimed. "There it will be."

"Will you come with me?"

"I'll be there shortly. Now go ahead and get a little hit start." He gestured toward the baggie, both suggesting and waiting for me.

I had thought earlier about how I could manage to pretend I was snorting the powder without inhaling a fatal dose of whatever he'd given me. I turned my back to him and laid out a line on the armrest of the sofa beside me. I looked at the decades-old filth on the fabric's malodorous covering that might once have been a muslin blend. If the drug didn't kill me, whatever else I'd be ingesting off this nasty piece of furniture would likely do the trick. What could I do? I ran my nose along the length of the line, breathing in loudly, all the while brushing most of the magic elixir away from my face and onto the nearest cushion. I hoped he wouldn't see.

"Excellent," he beamed. I turned to him with a fake look of serenity I'd plastered on my face. "Now, go and take your place. I'll get with you later for the rest of your payment." I nodded my agreement and took off toward the falls. I hoped like hell it wouldn't be my final resting place.

When I was sure I was out of sight and sound, I pulled out my phone and speed-dialed Paige. I'd earlier received a text that she'd been unsuccessful in her endeavor and had gone to the station for an urgent meeting.

***

"It just doesn't make sense," Turner voiced her consternation as she pored over the toxicology reports with her fellow detectives, who were noticeably keeping their distance from her. "There was no trace of drugs found in any of the first four victims. So, how did they die? And why would the killer change his MO midspree?"

The phone in her pocket vibrated. The buzzing might have offered some much-needed relief if her pockets had been a little deeper. She pulled it out and looked at the screen.

"Excuse me for a minute. I need to take this," Turner left the room and went out into the hallway in search of a little quiet and privacy. "This is a pleasant surprise."

"Sorry to cut you off when your voice is absolutely dripping with honey like the sweetest sopapilla." *Qué imagen. Did I just say that? Unbelievable.* "I don't have time to devote to dulce delights whispered in my ear. I might have to cut the call at any time, so listen carefully. I think I've got him, or well, maybe he's got me. I was just propositioned by a guy to play dead near Staircase Falls. Do you know where that is?"

"I don't have a clue. Why are you putting yourself in such danger? That wasn't our plan."

"We don't have time for that right now. You can bitch at me all you want, later. I'm headed to the water gardens on the river near the Grand Río hotel. Looks like a mini-Mayan temple. That's where he wants me. He tried drugging me. I tried to avoid as much of it as I could, but I'm sure some of it made it into my system, so if I say anything I shouldn't, just know I'm not to blame."

"I'm on my way."

Turner threw the door open and stuck her head back in the conference room long enough to tell her team what was happening. On the way to their vehicles, they made plans for who would go where. Thankfully, they were all out of uniform and dressed appropriately for the evening. On the way, Turner thought over how to go about things. She didn't want to put Bobbi's life in danger, yet they couldn't afford to let this guy get away. Thankfully, an idea came to her almost immediately.

***

"Take your clothes off," Turner whispered in a forceful way.

"Eeeewwwwww. I kinda like you this way." I batted my eyes flirtatiously.

"We don't have time to fool around. We need to switch clothes. I'm going to take your place."

I looked at her. "You don't think he's gonna notice that you're not me?"

"Hopefully, not until we've surrounded him and he's got no escape." Turner tightened the clothing closer to her body and snuggled into the greenery. "Now get out of here. One of my fellow officers is in the hotel's breezeway, waiting to take you to the hospital so you can get checked out. I want to make sure you're okay."

I stood and took a look around, wanting to make sure the man who was leaving me for dead wasn't on his way, which would ruin everything.

I decided to take advantage of a supposedly drug-induced moment. I took Turner's hand and whispered, "Be careful, please," to the woman who was risking all by taking my place.

***

Turner waited and waited. She wondered if she'd been made, if they'd been seen swapping clothes. She waited until almost sunrise. An early-morning jogger saw what he thought was a lifeless body laying half in the water, half in the gardens and let out a bloodcurdling scream.

Just in case he was watching, they played it to the hilt. An ambulance came, and emergency personnel behaved as though a true crime had taken place.

Once Turner was in the back of the ambulance, she rose from the gurney and stretched. She'd been stiff for hours. Her crime-busting colleagues were there with her. They'd been posing as EMTs.

Now what? was the question no one even bothered posing. They had no idea what to do next. They agreed to reconvene after they'd all had a chance to sleep on it.

***

Later that night, or was it morning? Who knew? I was so confused. I'd been cleared by a medical professional after the mini-high that kicked in at the hospital was all but gone. I found myself at Turner's place, with no recollection of how that had come to be.

92

I stirred from the couch where I'd been stretched out, and my hostess promptly appeared by my side with a glass containing a clear beverage.

"Are you trying to liquor me up?" I waggled my brows and took a drink. Disappointing. "*Agua* is all I get after such a harrowing experience?" I soon changed my playful tune, after seeing Turner's look of complete seriousness.

"What is it? What happened?"

"Nothing. I don't know. He never showed, and I'm not sure what that means. There's got to be something, other than him, that we're not seeing." Turner walked back to the desk where she'd been working, apparently still racking her brain.

I saw this as my chance to maybe get an answer to a burning curiosity. "Speaking of not seeing... Until all of this, I don't recall having ever seen you around. Are you new in town?" Turner relaxed and seemed to welcome the momentary distraction from her draining duty. She nodded and sat beside me. "So what, or who, brought you to the River City?"

"It's a long story."

"Sounds like one you're not too keen on sharing," I stated astutely.

Turner looked away from the label she'd been peeling from the bottle in her hand. Her fingers tightened on the glass.

"There was this woman..."

"There always is."

Chapter Fourteen

A FEW HOURS LATER, after we'd both finally gotten some sleep, Paige shared the morning paper with me.

Sixth Body Dispels Myth of May 5th

A sixth body was discovered after River Walk merchants and visitors were finally beginning to relax. Found on the Staircase Waterfall, near the Grand Río early Thursday morning, the body left little more than the murderer's penchant for our homeless population as evidence. San Antonio Police and Park Police have increased their patrols of the river and protection of the downtown area's homeless community, still searching for the culprit's identity.

They had to get some fake news in print so the killer would think his only witness was now among the deceased. Of course, that also meant that my days and nights of undercover work, a.k.a. being the bait, were over. No matter how alluring I could be.

When I finished reading about myself, I folded the paper and turned to Paige. "You know, I was watching *Forensic Files* the other night …"

Paige's eyebrows lifted and the right side of her mouth quirked at my admission.

"Hey. Don't judge. It's an extremely educational viewing experience." I paused to lick the barbecue sauce from my sticky fingertips. "Anyway, there was this case involving succinylcholine, and it got me to thinking about how easy it might be for someone to get away with murder by choosing drug addicts as victims. People whose arms are already riddled with needle marks wouldn't arouse any undue suspicions."

"Even if that were how it happened, we're still no closer to knowing whodunit, are we?"

We were enjoying a semirelaxing brunch on the patio in Paige's backyard, brainstorming theories. I decided to keep throwing mine on the floor and offered one that refused to be silenced in my mind. "What if there's more than one person doing the killing? And, what if there's more than one reason?"

Paige cocked her head to the side. "Keep talking. I'm listening."

"Let's say, for instance, that the three-piece-suit mystery man is involved, but only with the first four bodies, and that the motive was connected to the letters we all received."

"Okay. Go on."

"Unfortunately, that's where my thoughts run into a dead end."

"Just keep thinking out loud."

"Maybe there's a sicko psycho out there, who hates the homeless for some reason, and saw this as an opportunity."

"You mean like a copycat?"

I nodded. "Possibly. Or maybe the media is involved. The newspaper seems to be the only business profiting around here these days. I know I'm reaching—"

"No. You might be onto something."

***

Turner decided to pay a visit to the publisher of The Sentinel. She went out of uniform, so as not to attract attention to her visit.

"Believe me when I say that an increase in sales would neither directly affect nor serve as an incentive for any staff member to go on a killing spree. I can't possibly see how that could be a motive."

Turner hadn't expected the lead to turn into anything and was already thanking the man for his time and preparing to leave. He stopped her with a startling revelation.

"However, one of our reporters *is* in the middle of a multi-story exposé on the homeless. He's got high hopes for a shot at an award in journalism. I suppose I'd be remiss if I failed to mention his temper. He blew a gasket in the newsroom, just the other day, when a coworker wanted him to lower the volume on that noise he calls music."

Turner pulled out her pad and pen. "Can I get his name?"

Edwards smiled. "I can do you better than that. He's here now. Let me call him in here, and you can see what he's got to say."

A few minutes later, he opened the door and told Jameson, "Go on in." Of course, he hadn't told him who was waiting for him.

"Kevin Jameson?"

"Who wants to know?"

Turner showed him her badge, which he scrutinized carefully.

"I'm sure you know all about the murders along the river. I've seen your byline on at least one of the articles."

"Yeah, we all know about what's been happening. It'd be pretty sad if we didn't, wouldn't it? I mean, we *are* a newspaper."

Turner smiled in an attempt to disarm his defensive attitude, before realizing it appeared to be his nature. "Have a seat, please. I don't expect to keep you away from your work for long, but there's no point in you being uncomfortable during our conversation."

"Conversation? Don't you mean interrogation? What's this about anyway? Why do you want to talk to me? And apparently, only me."

"I'm following any and all leads in the case. I've recently come upon some information that I thought warranted a little closer investigation. I understand you're working on an editorial piece about the plight of the homeless in the city."

Jameson nodded.

"Can you tell me how your interest in that particular population came to be?"

Jameson narrowed his eyes and lifted his chin before responding, "Walk with me and take a look out the window. You'll see what I see every night and day. They're all over the place. I can't escape."

Turner followed him to his cubicle and looked out the glass to the streets below. There were lots of people about, and traffic bustled around the city's blocks.

"See what I mean."

Unable to shake the uneasiness caused by the interesting way he described his situation, Turner requested, "Can you get me a copy of all of the articles that have run in the series already?"

"Sure, but what do you hope to find between my unwritten lines?" Jameson smiled his challenge. When Turner failed to provide the response he seemed to be fishing for, he reached under his desk, grabbed a pile of papers, and handed them her way.

"That was fast and convenient."

"I'm still in the middle of writing the series, so I keep all of the copies handy."

Turner glanced at the dates at the top of the pages.

"I know what you're thinking. Bad timing on my part. I've been running a little low on the luck of the Irish. What can I say?"

Turner eyed him a bit suspiciously. "If I have any questions, I'm sure you won't mind if I pay you another visit."

"Of course not, by all means."

Turner prepared to leave.

"By the way. I wasn't going to say anything, and it's probably nothing, but I was in one of the tunnels recently, scouting around. I was trying to rouse a good angle, a focus, for my next piece, when another reporter suddenly walked in."

Turner cast a skeptical eye his way.

"Flynn. Derek Flynn. I didn't know what to make of his being there. I'm not sure what he was doing. I never saw any of it come out in the paper, so just a little food for thought."

"Thank you for your time, Mr. Jameson. And for the information. Hopefully, I won't need to see you again."

The man laughed loudly. "My, my, Officer. I get the impression that you mean that."

It was Turner's time to smile sardonically.

***

"Okay, let's talk this through," I said.

"This?"

"Yes, this." I eased back onto the sofa and got comfortable. This call would likely take some time. "Your hackles have been raised since you talked to this guy, Jameson."

"Oh. That this. There's something about his near obsession with the homeless, not philanthropic or even just because of his writing. I've watched him since our confrontation at the newspaper office. I couldn't tell you how many times I've seen him staring out that window facing Seguin Park. Almost like a lord watching over the peasants of his fiefdom. I don't know."

"Do you think maybe he's just watching them for inspiration for his writing?"

"If it were anyone else, I'd consider the possibility, but..."

"He just kinda sets off bells and alarms. He sorta creeps you out, doesn't he?"

Paige couldn't help but laugh at my shrewd synopsis. "I gathered copies of the stories he's been writing, the series on the homeless."

"And...?"

"I don't know. Maybe I'm reading way too much into it, but something just doesn't seem right."

"Keep talking."

"I don't know. I guess, I expected someone who chose the homeless as his research subject would show a little more empathy and compassion."

"Don't forget, *es periodista*. Aren't they supposed to be neutral and unbiased?"

"When they're writing news stories, yes. But his is a series of feature stories on the Op/Ed pages."

"Ah. Gotcha."

"Anyway."

"You know, I once saw an episode of a show that will remain unnamed, so as not to incite undue mockery." I grinned to myself. "The killer, who was a journalist, killed so he'd have something big and interesting to write about." When she got quiet, I explained. "Pardon my language, but you can't make this shit up, and neither can I. It's a true crime story. It's kinda like how some firefighters set fires so they can put them out, you know, fight flames for glory."

"I've read about the phenomenon. Some do it to create their chance to be a hero, others for the hazard pay, an increase in money."

"How big a deal is the Pulitzer Prize? What's it worth anyway?"

"Not sure, let me check it. You know what they say, one man's trinket is another man's treasure. It could be worthless as far as monetary value, but if it's important to him, that would make it priceless."

Computer keys clacked maniacally on both ends of the communication.

As I scrolled, I shared, "I read a book once, about a young man who made repeated attempts to travel from somewhere in Central America, Honduras I think it was, trying to reach his mother here in the States. She had left her family in search of the dream, or at least enough money to send back home for food and the necessities of life. His journey was so dangerous. For much of it, he rode on top of what they call the Train of Death. I think about it from time to time when I pass through Sabinal. *La migra* is always there at the railroad crossing. Anyway, the book was written after a series detailing this boy's travels appeared in the LA Times. The woman who wrote the articles won the Pulitzer for feature writing."

"Sorry to interrupt you, but it says here there is a $15,000 cash award for twenty categories of writing."

"Guess that would be enough to incite violence."

"People have killed for far less."

"So, what are we gonna do about it?"

"We, or at least the you part of the we, are going to stay safely out of it."

"Don't kick me to the curb just yet, Sherlock. I haven't reminded you about the other guy."

"What other guy?"

"Didn't Jameson rat out another staff writer to you?"

I could tell she'd completely forgotten about the second journalist.

***

Finally, the night of the Seether concert was upon them. Jameson and Flynn had agreed to drive together and left from the newspaper office.

"I hope you like steak," Flynn announced, as they pulled to the valet stand at Bohanan's.

"Are you kidding me? When I agreed to grab a bite to eat beforehand, I was thinking maybe The Republic of Texas or something similar, at the most expensive. I can't afford this place."

Flynn smiled. "No worries, man. I got it covered. My mom's a wine seller and gets gift cards for lots of fancy food. She's always giving them to me. My parents live in Anaqua Springs, and they don't like to come downtown much anymore. They prefer to drive to Boerne instead. Lucky me. Have a look see." He opened his wallet and showed Jameson several gift cards bulging in front of the bills he carried there.

"You sure live large, dude."

"I like to indulge occasionally. Since we were headed this way, I thought it would be the perfect opportunity to finally use one of these babies."

"Must be nice." Jameson smiled big, as they were shown to their table. He looked over the impressive menu. They didn't want to be late, so they ordered immediately. Flynn decided on a ribeye filet with a baker, and Jameson settled on a New York Strip with asparagus and au gratin potatoes.

They relaxed in their seats after the waiter left them. Flynn raised his glass. "To friendship," he toasted Jameson.

"To friendship. Great music. And even better writing." Jameson smiled broadly.

***

Their plates were cleared, and they were waiting for the bill. "So what did you think?" Flynn asked.

"It's easily the most exquisitely cooked red meat I've ever eaten. And the potatoes were amazing."

Flynn laughed. "Yeah, I don't think theirs come from a Betty Crocker pouch. So, we good now?"

"Dude, we were good before, even without all this. I told you; it's all good."

Flynn had his reasons for wanting to believe that.

He led Jameson past a long line of people in front of the theatre, like a VIP. Ignoring the hostile looks and unkind words overheard, they showed their passes at the door and were immediately allowed entry. Their seats for the concert were in the front row, and they had access to the musician's dressing rooms.

While they waited for the signal that it was their time to meet and greet the band members, they prepared for their interview by sharing what they already knew about the musicians and their music.

Flynn had been tasked with writing the piece. He quizzed Jameson, "So, what's your favorite Seether song?"

"That's easy. Most definitely 'Broken.'"

"Because?"

"Because Amy Lee." Jameson smiled at his own reference to the Evanescence singer and one-time girlfriend of Seether's front man and lead singer. "And because of the message, the instrumentation. I don't know. I guess the lyrics resonate with me."

"So, what do you think Seether fans would want to know? Hurry, we don't have much time before they give us our few minutes of fame."

"Where they get the inspiration for their lyrics. I don't know. Aren't you a fan?"

"I'm more of an 'Outside' Staind kinda guy myself, but I do know 'Broken.'"

"So, go with that."

They both looked, when the door opened to a man dressed in all black, with a wireless headset. After making eye contact, he motioned. "You're on. You've got ten minutes, maybe fifteen, tops."

"Thanks." They hurried in.

***

Far from a front-page piece, Flynn got a paragraph and small photo inside the entertainment section. Both he and Jameson came away with signed, backstage passes and a few CDs. While Seether's annual music festival to raise money for suicide awareness was well-known among fans, Flynn latched onto the depth of emotion that served as a catalyst for the event's creation. He spent most of his time probing with personal inquiries that allowed him a glimpse of the softer side and more private nature of the South African, post-grunge, alternative metal, band member.

***

It was late in the day by the time Paige got to take a good look at the paper. The fact that she finally had a few minutes for such a luxury should have been her first clue that all hell was about to break loose. It didn't hit her until she made it to the Op/Ed page and her eyes landed on a familiar face. She looked twice, then three times, just to be sure. *Thanks be to God that photo isn't attached to an obituary.*

The byline next to Dottie's photo caught her eye immediately. Her hackles were raised. She didn't believe in coincidence, so she read with a discerning mind and watchful eyes.

HOME IS WHERE THE SHOPPING CART IS

by Kevin Jameson

Dorothy Brown, known to her friends as Dottie, is no stranger to San Antonio's homeless community. She's been on the downtown streets since her New Orleans birthplace was deluged by Hurricane Katrina in 2005. The city opened shelters for those left homeless and displaced by the flooding. It soon became a way of life for the Cajun Lady.

When asked about that particular experience, she shared, "It was bad, real bad. So many people lost their lives, their homes. Others their families. Me, I didn't have much to lose. I always was a minimalist, and it finally worked to my advantage."

While most homeless fill their carts with what little clothing they have and any treasures they find on the streets, Dottie is...well, different, the exception, you might say. Dottie's cart has more books than blouses, more paperbacks than pants. Dottie loves to read.

"I fell in love with books when I was a little girl and my momma used to take me to the public library. I still go to the one here, only

without an address, I can't check books out to read. All of these, in my cart, were unwanted throwaways. Kinda like me."

A well-read woman, over the years, Dottie has amassed an impressive vocabulary, which many who take the time to listen to what the woman has to say find surprising and fascinating.

"I guess some people equate not having a permanent place of residence with not having a brain. Sure, there are homeless here under the bridges who waste their lives and minds on drugs and drinking, but there are lots of others here who are simply going through some hard times. Believe it or not, there are people here with college degrees, who once made six-figure salaries. Everybody has a reason. We all have a story."

Dottie stopped there and inquired if I wanted to hear more of her story.

"I'm from New Orleans' Lower Ninth Ward, originally. I was one of the many bused here after the hurricane. I didn't have a home before I left the city, so I had nothing to go back to. What's the difference, being homeless there or here? It's pretty much all the same."

Her eyes lit from behind with mischief in the making. "I suppose I'd be telling a different story if I'd been homeless on a Hawaiian island or some other tropical paradise."

Most people wouldn't expect a homeless person to know much about travel and such places, but, Dottie does. She's different, remember, out of the ordinary.

"I never felt afraid here, until recently. All those killings going on. Somebody's got a bone to pick with my people, and I don't understand their reasoning. What on earth have we done to be sacrificed in such a way?"

As you might imagine, it's challenging for people like Dottie to find a source of income so necessary to change their situation. "Who in their right mind is going to give me a job? Just look at me. Would you hire me?"

But there are resources available to the homeless community, shelters that offer beds and kitchens that provide meals. And there are volunteer organizations that make it their mission to spread the word about their many offerings. Dottie shared that she recently met a wonderfully warm and nice woman who spent some time getting to know her. "It's the little things like that that make a life worth living."

Paige's cellphone vibrated.

"Are you reading what I'm reading?"

Uncanny. Bobbi and I seemed to be in sync in many ways. "I find the timing of the story suspect. It makes me feel terribly uneasy."

"Why's that?"

"I just spent some time with this woman, Dottie, talking to her in that place. Makes me wonder if he was there, if he saw us, saw me. Is this story his way of making some sort of a statement? Or sending me a message?"

"Was that you she was talking about?"

"Maybe."

"*¿Dónde estás?*"

"Right now? I'm at home."

"Do you know where he is?"

"No. Holy shit! I'd better get over there now. Thanks again."

"You know, you need to watch more ID TV. Just sayin'."

***

A few hours later, Paige sent Bobbi a text.

For my peace of mind, I've put Dottie up at a motel for a few days. Hopefully this nightmare will soon be over. I feel like we're getting close, like we're maybe just missing another piece or two of the puzzle.

Now that she had Dottie tucked safely out of harm's reach, Paige explored her curiosity as to whether there might be a connection between the two newsmen. She decided to look into the other half of the dynamic duo, Derek Flynn.

It was obvious that the younger Flynn was blessed, at least financially. His father, Michael Flynn, was a wealthy corporate executive. By all accounts, he appeared to lead an extremely predictable and routine life for a man of his means. Married with children, well, at least one child. Derek was heir to the dynasty. The family lived comfortably in a well-to-do suburb, close enough for convenience, yet far enough away for peace, quiet, and privacy. Turner looked at the photographs she'd unearthed. Apparently, the man liked to golf. He hung out with his monied cronies at country clubs and hosted swanky dinner parties at his imposing estate.

She clicked on a link to a site that took her to *Luxury Home Magazine* and a slide of images that began with a two-story, Mediterranean with a three-car garage, fronted by gorgeously carved wooden doors, behind which she expected nothing less than the shine of German and Italian imports. She read the descriptions that accompanied each of the photographs: *magazine-worthy architectural details including mesquite hardwood floors, alder wood details, a striking, hand-built floating staircase.* She had to admit, it was pretty and impressive. The home backed to a dedicated park situated atop one of the highest peaks in Anaqua Springs. The word grandiose came unbidden to mind. For a minute, she entertained the fantasy that she was the Flynn's invited guest. *Nah, not my style.*

She looked, once more, at the photos she'd found and the smiling visage of the top executive for Pickens Petroleum. Michael Flynn had dedicated his professional life to the company. She just couldn't fathom any possible connection to poverty or homelessness that anyone in this family might have. The Houston Chronicle listed a staggering salary for the man. In her lifetime, she'd never earn near what he made in a year.

She would have a talk with Flynn, the younger, but didn't expect much. She couldn't see him with a motive. A silver spoon in his mouth, or maybe even a 14K gold one, but no reason to kill. She suspected he was given everything he wanted and needed, and more.

***

While she wasn't sure what she expected, Turner was surprised when she met Derek Flynn. He hadn't appeared in any of the pictures she'd found, and she'd falsely assumed he'd be a Mini-Me of his Daddy Warbucks. He looked nothing like his father. Whether he'd prove to be a good or bad apple, he'd fallen far from the tree. The young man with long brown hair, tattoos, and piercings had an extremely engaging smile and immediate likability.

"Hello, Officer." He extended his hand to her. "I'm Derek Flynn. I understand you have a few questions for me."

"Yes, Mr. Flynn. This shouldn't take long." She waited for the editor to vacate the premises. "A witness has come forward with testimony that puts you at the scene of a crime, and I'm duty-bound to ask you about it."

Flynn tilted his head and bit his bottom lip. A look of concerned confusion replaced his affable smile. "Okay. Where? And when?"

"Last Tuesday, May 10, under the San Pedro overpass."

He remained silent, as if trying to track back in the calendar of his mind. *Is he stalling for time, concocting a cover story of some kind?* Turner watched him closely and carefully for any of deception's tell-tale signs. As if he had found what he was looking for, his face glowed with certainty. *Was that an alibi in formation?*

"Yes. I remember now. I was bummed that night because the Seguin Park lead had been compromised. I didn't think whoever was responsible for the murders would be foolish enough to return there, so I set out for the most obvious and nearest encampment of homeless people. I headed for the San Pedro overpass, the concrete tunnels that run under Highway 281."

"What did you do there?"

"I spoke to a few people. I was trying to find out if they'd seen anyone who seemed out of place the last few nights."

"And?"

"One of the ladies, a real friendly one, described a man that sounded an awful lot like Jameson, one of the other staff writers here. Sure enough, a story about her appeared in the paper a few days later. Just today was it? Anyway, I didn't think more about it."

"Did anyone else offer any useful information?"

"No. As a matter of fact, I remember leaving there feeling discouraged and out of ideas."

"You weren't looking to solve a crime?"

"No ma'am. I was looking for a lead on a story. Something I could write."

"What did you do when you left the tunnel?"

"I came back here for a little while. We were on deadline. After that, I went home."

"Can you give me an idea of time for those movements? It doesn't have to be exact, roundabouts will be fine."

***

Dottie would soon corroborate Flynn's accounting, as would several other office mates. Apparently, he was trying to enlist the help of any and most every one of them for ideas and inspiration that night.

Frustrated by the realization that she'd reached another dead end, Turner found herself back at square one again. She put her pen and pad away, breathed a heavy sigh, and headed for home.

Chapter Fifteen

PAIGE SAID SHE NEEDED some time to think and someone to help her accomplish that goal. She said it was seeming more and more natural to call me.

"Do you think you can get away for an hour or two?"

I looked around at the empty tables that surrounded me. "I think I can swing it. Especially if there's a possibility for a little afternoon delight."

"I swear, woman," Paige growled, but I could hear the smile in her voice. "Meet me at your back door. I'll be there in about ten minutes."

After disconnecting from the call, my thoughts turned toward how the nature and comfort level of our relationship was changing. I blatantly flirted with her now, and that made my heart happy.

"I wasn't expecting a police cruiser. Should I get in the back seat behind the steel mesh screen and bulletproof glass?"

"Shut up and get in. I swear, woman." Paige was laughing.

"You seem to be swearing a lot these days. So, what's this all about?"

"I just need to think, and you help me with that. I need you."

I swallowed the lump of what I would like that to mean.

"Where are you taking me? Apparently, I'm a prisoner of your whims. Perhaps someday, I'll be one of your *deseos y fantasías*."

Paige lowered her chin and looked at me over the top of her dark lenses. She pulled into the lot of the Japanese Tea Garden in Brackenridge Park. "This place works for me. I find the zen atmosphere relaxing, conducive to profound thinking. And we can have lunch while we're here."

"Sounds good to me."

We strolled the grounds and sat by the koi ponds, even watched an origami demonstration. The shaded walkways, stone bridges, and waterfall all helped to calm our senses.

"I realize it's only been a few days, or has it been weeks?" I laughed out loud at the realization. "But I've often found myself wondering what you're like when you're not under so much stress and tension," I looked at Paige, whose hair was twisted in a tight knot at the back of her head. "You know, when you let your hair down."

"I'm afraid if this doesn't end soon, I won't have any left to let down."

I smiled sadly with pursed lips. "I wish I could help you out."

"You have. You do. You are. I love bouncing thoughts and theories off you, just being with you. I don't have any friends here in San Antonio, at all."

"If you recall, I tried to get you to talk to me about that, but you cut that convo short immediately."

Paige laughed. "I had just moved here when the body was found in the river. As a matter of fact, it was the day before I first stopped in at your place. I still haven't finished unpacking."

I reflected on the memory before asking, "Where'd you come from?"

"Not far, but far enough. I was up in Frisco, near Dallas."

"I've only been once, when I accompanied my partner at the time on a business trip for a quick getaway. It's nice there. Different. Expensive, but much less... colorful, should we say? What were you doing there?"

Paige smiled before I remembered aloud, "Oh that's right, there was this woman."

We both laughed, and finally, Paige divulged a little more about her previous relationship. "Her name was Sarah. We met in Juneau. That's where I'm from."

"Wow. As in Alaska? You're a long way from home."

"Tell me about it. Anyway, I pulled her over for speeding one day, and well, the rest and we are now history."

"¡Ay Dios mío! The stories we think only happen in books and on TV."

Paige stood and we walked. Out of necessity, our conversation turned back toward the killings, as we made our way toward Jingu House. While we both opted for chicken stir fry, I chose spicy sriracha and Paige the sesame yakitori. Both were served with Asian noodles, a California roll, and salad. I ordered crab and cucumber and Paige wanted to try the ginger lime. Since it was a weekday, there weren't that many people around, so we got our food to go and carried it to the pavilion.

We were quiet for the first few minutes of our eating, until suddenly a thought occurred to me. Despite fearing reproachful recriminations, I shared it with Paige, "You know, *la otra noche* I was listening to *Crime Stories with Nancy Grace*." I waited for a comment, but Paige seemed to be accepting my IDiosyncratic viewing and listening behaviors. "The episode was about this serial killer in Florida who targeted the homeless population. All the psychological profiling and such was interesting, but it got me to thinking. I'm not sure that's what's happening here."

Paige looked at me quizzically, so I explained. "I mean, yes, whoever is doing the killing is definitely targeting homeless people, but I'm not so sure it has anything to do with the fact that they're homeless other than that their situation makes them easy to use. Are you with me?" Paige nodded. "I guess what I'm trying to say is that if we focus on that part of the puzzle, I'm afraid we're going to miss the bigger and more important part of the picture needed to solve the mystery. Maybe the why will lead us to who. Does that make sense to you?"

Paige nodded again. "It does, but I think I need to let your words rearrange and settle in my brain before I can help them form any more viable and helpful theories." We stood to leave and gathered our waste to recycle. "Thanks, as always."

But I couldn't take the credit and wanted to give props where they were due. "If it helps, it's Charlie you'll need to thank. He's the one that cautioned against the misconception."

* * *

Later that evening, on stage at Rainbow Reads, Charlie was hosting a local author for a pre-Pride reading. Judging by the novels on her display, the woman wrote under two different pen names: Marilyn Mujer and Ann Ahnimus Rhiter. Who knew her real name? As her host for the event, Charlie was ashamed to admit he hadn't had time to read a paragraph from any of them. She was promoting her latest release, a book about cowgirls and rodeos. That would explain the preponderance of western wear on the women in attendance.

After introducing the writer, Charlie took a copy of the book from the signing table and turned to the back cover for the synopsis. When he finished reading it, he flipped it back over to admire the cover art. Once Marilyn, or Ann, or whoever she was finished thanking everyone for spending a little of their evening with her, Charlie put the book in his lap and gave her his full attention. The author set the scene.

"This, my latest novel"—She held high a paperback with a photograph of two cowgirls on the cover—"tells the tale of two women who've been burned by recent relationships. I think some of us can relate. I know I can." Many in the audience nodded and laughed, knowingly. "The part I'm going to read takes place after the women, both rodeo participants, have met and shared their stories. They've commiserated. There's definitely an attraction heating between them, but they're both a little gun shy and trying not to give in." More laughter. "In this passage, Kendall, who is a barrel racer, has convinced Deb, a roper, to show her how to throw a lasso and catch a steer. Let me just read the passage. Afterward, maybe you can let me know what you think."

Chapter Sixteen

UNKNOWN TO ME, OFFICER Paige Turner had eased into the last row of chairs sometime during the author's initial greeting. She'd moved forward at the end, as women waited in line to get their books signed. I felt the warm caress of her breath on my neck, so unexpected I was nearly panting out loud. She whispered over my shoulder, "We have to stop meeting like this or tongues are going to wag. I thought you were working this evening?"

"Uh...hello. I could say the same about you." I turned to face her.

Paige smiled. "I am. Just taking a break."

"So, what'd you think?"

"I definitely have a new appreciation for cowgirls and rodeoing."

I laughed and confessed, "Sometime I'll have to share my fascination for roping and riding." Paige smiled, and we walked out into the night with our signed books.

"Clearly, you've been holding out on me. How'd you manage a night off? Who's running Beta's?"

"Sadly, it's been slow lately, so I'm letting the girls have a go at handling it on their own."

"Billie and Bety?"

"Yeah. They've expressed an interest in going into the business after they graduate, so they've gotta get their feet wet sometime. What about you?"

"I haven't had dinner yet. I just stopped in for the reading."

"Neither have I."

"Sounds like it's a date." Paige winked at me. "So where should we go? What do you feel like eating?"

Now, that's a loaded question. "Together, twice in the same day? Careful now, you could make a girl feel special that way."

Paige smiled before glancing at her watch. "I'm sorry to say I don't have much time. I'm heading back to the bridge or tunnel, and I'm not yet dressed for the occasion." She gestured to her clothing.

We had stopped next to the outdoor tables of a restaurant and a woman carrying menus was already headed our way. Yes, desperate times called for desperate measures. It looked like she was going to do everything in her power to make sure we didn't get away. "Well, here we are at one of the best barbeque spots on the river. Are you game?"

"I don't know. You tell me. Do you think we can handle adding any more sauce to our flirtation?"

I barked a huge laugh in response to her rhetorical question.

Not long after, we found ourselves seated beneath an umbrella styled like a red, white, and blue Texas flag. Clearly unable to decide, Paige stared blindly at the menu and bought some time with a question. "Do you ever feel like you're taking food out of your mouth when you eat out?"

I laughed. "Believe me. I get tired of cooking and look forward to it. Now, stop stalling and choose something."

"I'm sorry. As hungry as I am and as much as I know I need to hurry, I don't know what I want. What are you having?"

"Brisket and beans. In my opinion, it's their best plate."

"Sounds good to me. I'll have the same."

"Wow. Are you always this easy?" I batted my eyes playfully, and Paige blushed profusely.

Once our orders were placed, we relaxed into a nice conversation.

"I grew up in a small town. So small I couldn't wait to get out of it," Paige shared.

"In Alaska, right?"

"Yes. My dad, well step, was in the Coast Guard. His last port of call was on the Inside Passage."

"Was it that bad? I mean, as someone who was born and raised in a city of over a million people, I often find myself wishing I'd had a different experience."

"Oh, I guess it was fine when I was a kid. Before my libido kicked in. Can you imagine? Everyone knew everyone, and the lesbian pool was a little on the shallow side, at least of those who weren't afraid to admit they liked girls. Even when I got a little older, I always felt like I was participating in a swap meet every time I went on a date."

I grinned.

"I'm serious. Before the movie ended, or we were done with dinner, the conversation always came around to exes. Sure enough, there were far less than six degrees of separation between any of us. You couldn't swing a dyke without hitting someone one of you had gone out with or down on."

I sprayed my beer out at that. I laughed so hard, and this time, Paige joined in.

"Remember the woman, Sarah, the one I mentioned? The one I told you I stopped for speeding?"

I nodded. *Of course I remembered.*

"Well, she was only visiting Juneau. She lived here in Texas. She let it be known, right away, that she wasn't interested in and wouldn't consider relocating. Foolish me, I follow my heart no matter where it leads me. So, here I am. End of story."

I was enjoying getting to know Paige this way. I was realizing that, as our relationship grew closer, less professional and more personal, I thought of her more by her first name and not her last. *Interesting.*

"Did you ever think that maybe this Sarah was just a means to an end? Maybe you were supposed to come to Texas for some reason. Maybe it was all part of the plan of some higher being. But you must have thought your relationship would last, I mean to go such a distance."

"I did."

"You know, I had you pegged as a heartbreaker from the get go."

"Did you now? And what makes you think I'm not the one who got her heart broken?" The inside corners of her eyebrows were slanting upward as she looked at me. "But enough about me. How about you? It's your turn." She used her fork to spear a tine full of pinto beans and held them my way. "So, spill them already."

I finished chewing before answering. "Well, as you might imagine, in a city this size, there's no dearth of ways to meet people. The problem is, not all women who go to the clubs, even on lesbian night, are gay. Some go for the music, others to be out with their purely platonic girlfriends for a good time without men around. And there are always those who are questioning, interested in experimenting. That's how and where I met Lauren, who fit best into the last category."

"Do you feel comfortable talking about her? I know you two were together for some time."

"How do you know that? I know I haven't told you about her. We haven't had time before tonight."

"I overheard your friends talking one night. Mother's Day it was. They came to be there with and for you. Talked about how the holiday always made you a little sad, because of the woman's daughter. Rachel, I think her name was?"

"That's right." I smiled. "I thought she was the one, Lauren that is. I guess because I wanted her to be. We were together for seven years, and that's about how old Rachel was when we met. Lauren moved out about three times, and I foolishly let her come back. I think, hope, it was only because of Rachel that I kept taking her back. Rachel was such a sweet kid. I felt bad for her, the way her mother was dragging her all over the country, following whatever man she hooked up with, until it didn't work out with him, and she'd come running back to me, again and again. Finally, I had enough of her using me. I haven't been with anyone since."

"How long ago did your relationship end?"

"That depends on your definition of end. If you're asking me when I last saw her, it was about five years ago. She tried to finagle an invitation to come by the house. She still calls from time to time. I don't answer or return the calls, and I certainly wouldn't let her in."

The sound of silence was deafening, so I quickly changed the subject, "Do you know what time it is?"

"I have a pretty good idea."

"Time flies when you're having fun."

"It sure does. Bobbi, please don't take this the wrong way, but I have to get going."

I nodded and tried to control the downward pull threatening the expression on my face.

"I've enjoyed our time together this evening and hope we can share more moments like this, soon."

"But, Cinderella's ball is about to end, and the Great Pumpkin is waiting."

Paige smiled, but her stare was empty. "I think you're mixing your animated images, but thanks for understanding."

We laughed as we made our way toward where Paige had parked.

"Well, this is me." Paige stopped next to a red motorcycle.

"Are you shitting me?" My eyes couldn't have grown any wider or my mouth dropped open any farther in surprise. "That's a pretty nice pumpkin you got there."

Paige couldn't wipe the ear-to-ear grin off her face. "Why does my personal mode of transportation surprise you?"

"I don't know. I just—"

"Have a thing for motorcycle mamas?" Paige laughed heartily. "You know, if it wasn't so late and we didn't both have work to do, I'd ask you to strap one on and climb on behind me."

"Strap one on, huh?" I waggled my eyebrows.

Paige laughed. "A helmet! Strap a helmet on. I keep a spare on the back. I swear."

I looked. Sure enough, there was one there, ready and waiting.

"Not that I wouldn't love to wrap my legs around your gas tank and slide my hoochie right behind your behind, but if I were to do that, even for a little ride, I'm afraid neither one of us would get done what we need to tonight." I reached out and touched Paige's arm affectionately. "Be safe out there. I'll be thinking of you and waiting to hear. Don't keep me worrying, no matter how late it gets. Promise?"

Paige put her hand over mine and gave it a gentle squeeze before she snapped her helmet and climbed on. She smiled and waved as she rode away. I watched her disappear into the distance. *"Si no te hubieras ido."* I smiled and shook my head before heading back to Beta's, where I found the girls taking care of business. Things were running smoothly, and I felt unneeded.

Wanting to both feel and be close to Paige, instead of going home, I headed to the station where I gave detailed information to a forensic sketch artist in a last-ditch effort to do my part for the community.

***

Armed with the description Bobbi had provided, which unfortunately fit most every Caucasian male in his mid-fifties to early sixties, Turner readied herself for her tunnel foray. A team of police took their standby places. There was one other detective under the bridge with her, far enough away to not appear suspicious, while close enough to offer any needed assistance should they get lucky.

She watched and waited. She thought she recognized an approaching male but he was still too far away to see clearly. He came slowly sauntering her way. He didn't walk directly to her but approached in more of a roundabout way, as if he hadn't already chosen her as his next victim. He didn't appear to be too much of a pro at this. Meanwhile, thanks to Bobbi's advice, she mimicked an addict's withdrawal behavior as best she could. She was so focused on acting that she almost missed the look of sheer disgust that briefly passed over the well-dressed man's face.

"Hello, beautiful." He finally stood beside her.

Turner couldn't believe it. She knew that face. Working hard to conceal her recognition, she scoffed, "Forget it mister. I'm not into blowjobs or flatbacks. I don't care how much you're paying. I'm sure you'll find someone desperate enough."

The man laughed heartily. "Oh my. Aren't we the feisty one? No sweat, sweetheart. I'm not here to solicit for sex or any kind of illicit favor."

It took every ounce of Turner's conviction to choke her desire to throttle the scumbag. She had to wait until he made the right move, one that would serve as more than circumstantial evidence. She wanted to make sure the case against him would be impenetrable and make it all the way through the sometimes flawed criminal justice system. "What are you looking for? Can't be anything good if you've resorted to the underground."

The man laughed again. "I noticed you were sniffling a little bit."

"So what? You a doctor? It's allergy season."

The man chose to ignore her distractions. "There's something I want, and I think there's something you need."

"A tissue, maybe?"

When the man failed to respond right away, Paige feared she'd pushed too hard and hurried to remedy the situation. "What do you want from me?"

The man, who appeared to have readied himself to walk away, stopped and looked at her. "I suppose you're aware of the bodies found along the river."

Paige recoiled a little, hoping he would see some small semblance of fear on her face.

"Don't worry, darling. Whoever was doing that, it wasn't me. But, I want to keep the scare going."

Paige cocked her head and looked at him.

***

Having grown tired and bored with looking at mugshots, I pulled out my phone and searched names I remembered from recent conversations. It wasn't long before I saw a face I recognized. I couldn't wait to share the news with Paige. Unfortunately, my call went straight to voicemail. I hoped like hell that Paige wasn't, at that moment, staring into that same face.

***

"All I want is for you to pretend to be dead until someone finds you and screams loud enough to get a reporter's attention and a story in the newspaper."

"But why? What does that get you?"

"Never you mind about that. I have my reasons."

"Okay, so what's in it for me?"

He pulled a clear baggie out of his pocket. "Enough of this for a week's worth of happy."

Paige smiled and reached for the bag. She grabbed the man's wrist and twisted his arm until he spun around with it pinned behind his back. She held him tightly, while blowing her ear piercing whistle. Her partner immediately came running her way.

As they walked him to the patrol car, Paige recited the Miranda warning, "You have the right to remain silent. Anything you say can and will be used against you in a court of law …"

***

Shortly after the suspect was brought in, Derek Flynn's well-compensated contact at the station called him.

"This better be good," Flynn grumbled into his phone.

"Oh, it is. And, it'll be worth every penny you're going to pay me."

"You're gonna have to give me more than that."

"A man suspected of being San Antonio's River Walk killer has been apprehended."

Flynn jumped out of bed and splashed water on his face. He grabbed some clothes, slammed a ball cap on his bedhead, and called his apartment's valet.

***

It had been almost an hour since he'd been photographed and fingerprinted, and Flynn had yet to utter a single word. All the while, Turner attempted to engage him in relaxed and hopefully fruitful conversation.

"You know, I talked to Derek just the other day."

At the mention of his son's name, Flynn finally met her gaze with daggers in his eyes. "You leave my son out of this. He had nothing to do with any of it."

Turner hoped the Achilles heel she appeared to have hit was connected to Flynn's mouth. Maybe, if she continued to push, a confession would fall out, or at least some useful information.

"He was seen coming out of the San Pedro homeless encampment around the time a victim was approached. Much in the same way you solicited me."

For a moment, Flynn appeared to stop breathing. The color drained from his face, and he stiffened visibly. "Must have been a case of mistaken identity. Besides, he is a staff writer for the newspaper. These incidents have generated much newsworthy attention of late. Outside of work, my son had no reason—"

"And what reason could you have possibly had?"

Flynn's face reddened with anger.

"Do you have children, Detective?" Flynn's chin trembled. Without giving her a chance to respond, he offered, perhaps unwittingly, a motive and reason. "Derek is my only son. There isn't anything in this world I wouldn't do for him. But neither a father's love, nor all the money he has to give, can provide everything."

Turner leaned forward. Flynn had lowered his voice, seemingly transported by his own thoughts.

"No matter what I did, how much I gave him, Derek never seemed satisfied or happy. He floundered without direction, both in his personal life and his career, which fell far short in its ability to fulfill him emotionally and support him financially. His mother and I were proud of him and would have stood by him, no matter what he did. We were committed to helping him find his way. Instead of appreciating our efforts, it was almost as if he resented them, resented us. Especially me."

Turner remained quiet and listened intently. The video recording would catch anything she might miss.

"It was only recently that he finally admitted to me that he was unsatisfied with what he was doing with his life. He felt like he was stuck in a professional rut, just spinning his wheels without getting anywhere. That's when I got an idea."

At that point, the door to the interrogation room burst open. A small man wearing a big Stetson followed his briefcase in.

"Stop right there, Michael. It's my advice as your attorney that you say nothing more until we've had an opportunity to speak privately."

"Oh, Arthur. Relax. I have nothing to hide. I don't see what's wrong with laying my cards on the table."

"Well, let me tell you what's wrong with that. One of those cards you turn over right now just might prove to be the river card. You know what that means, right? Please. Just wait. I can only help you if you'll let me."

Flynn ignored his lawyer's pleading, and Arthur Radcliff threw his hands in the air, signaling defeat. He shook his head and took a seat at the table, pulled a legal pad from his briefcase, and vigorously scribed notes with his Montblanc.

"I believe we were in the midst of discussing parenting, Officer. Were we not?"

Turner nodded.

"When it became apparent to me that Derek had no idea how to climb the ladder to the height he deserved as a Flynn, the thought occurred to me that maybe I could give him a little nudge. I could help him get noticed, move him along a little, professionally."

"Michael. Please. I'm begging you to stop. Please."

"After he confided in me that he wasn't even sure a newspaper writer was what he wanted to be, I thought maybe all he needed was a little push, a little something to get his writing on the front page. A story of substance would finally get him some attention."

"Michael. For the last time—"

"Arthur, give it a rest. You're making me regret I ever called you. She already knows what I did. I'm merely explaining my reason."

With a clenched jaw and pinched lips, Flynn's counsel again retreated.

"I thought perhaps a few headlines could give him the boost his ego needed. Thought maybe they'd catch the eyes of a publisher or two, who could lift him to where he should be. Someone with connections might help him excel at true crime writing."

Flynn accepted the glass of water that Turner slid across the table.

"I never meant to hurt anyone. It was my belief that only a person who already used drugs would be interested in my offerings, so what difference would it make? I honestly believed, in the end, they'd simply be able to walk away unscathed by the experience."

"But they didn't, did they? At least not all of them. Just how many were there?"

Radcliff shook his head, and for once, Flynn seemed to follow his lead.

"Let's see, if I remember correctly, the man in the river was the first," Turner prompted.

Flynn bolted upright out of the slouch he'd slid into during his storytelling. His voice was loud, strong, and adamant. "I had nothing to do with that man's drowning. Aside from you and the other undercover you mentioned, the only other person I engaged was the young man who was found in the river boat. To be honest, I did him a favor. Did you happen to see the condition he was in? Disgraceful to say the least." With his nose high in the air, Flynn practically snorted in disgust, as he reclaimed his sense of superiority.

Turner's dilated nostrils and icy stare threatened to reveal her true feelings. She shut off the recording and stood with a triumphant glare. "That's all we need."

* * *

As soon as Derek arrived, his contact told him, "He's lawyered up and refused to give his real name. He was smart enough not to carry a wallet or any identification on him, and his fingerprints gave us nothing on AFIS. But, as the luck of any Friday the thirteenth would have it, the officer who nabbed him knows who he is."

As if on cue, a door banged open, and a duo of officers entered the hall escorting a detained man. Flynn looked their way, then turned his attention back to the processing clerk. He shook his head as if to clear it of what he couldn't possibly have seen. He turned back toward the trio again.

"Dad? What are *you* doing here?"

The man turned to him. "Derek? I'm afraid there's been a terrible misunderstanding."

Paige looked back and forth between father and son, before turning to escort Michael Flynn to a temporary holding cell, where he would likely remain longer than he anticipated.

"Wait! Officer, there has to be an explanation. My father isn't a killer. Are you, Dad? Tell her. Say something. Anything." Derek blinked rapidly. Tears threatened, but not one escaped.

"Don't worry, son. Arthur is here. He'll take care of all of this. Now, go home and spend some time with your mother before she gets wind of this travesty of justice some other way."

Ironically, the other way would have ordinarily come from Derek himself. He sped north on Interstate 10, hoping to beat the television news crews who would soon be on their way. He'd gladly hand this story over to Jameson.

***

Naturally, the burning question in most minds was why wealthy Michael Flynn didn't just pay someone else to do his dirty work for him. Speculation was that he had, early on, then had to take care of business himself in the end. An unconventional and far from seasoned gambler, he had risked it all and faced years of confinement because of it.

Later, to other inquiring minds, Michael Flynn would repeat what he'd told Turner during his initial questioning. He hadn't ever wanted Derek to know that he'd had a hand in whatever promotion, new career, or accolades might come his way. As fate would have it, Derek found out in the worst possible and most shameful way.

Needless to say, Derek Flynn was emotionally and professionally devastated. He refused to believe his father could do such a thing. He was mortified, embarrassed, hurt, and ashamed. He'd never live down the humiliation of the headline, *Crime Reporter's Father Turns Criminal to Earn His One and Only Son's Fame*. Mr. Edwards, his editor, assured Derek that he held nothing his father had done against him, but Derek immediately turned in his resignation. For the time being, he knew his mother would desperately need him. At home with her was where he most needed to be.

The two of them would eventually leave the area to escape the notoriety.

Chapter Seventeen

AS PAIGE WOULD SOON learn, Mrs. Flynn wasn't the only mother who needed their child's closeness and comfort.

"Hey, Mom. To what do I owe this completely out of character initiation of communication?"

"What on earth are you talking about?"

"Well, I *am* always the one who calls you. You never call me."

"Oh, dear. That's only because your life is so much more filled than mine. I don't want to crash any of your parties."

"Uh-huh. So, what's going on?"

"I have the most wonderful news!"

Well, at least it sounds good.

"I've finally opened my heart again. I'm completely in love."

How did she feel about that, shocked? selfish? worried? likely all of the above. Paige couldn't believe what she was hearing. "Wait a minute. Didn't we just speak a few days ago?"

"We did, and it was after our talk that I realized just how lonely and unhappy I've been. You know how hard it's been on me, Paige, with your leaving and Philip's dying."

Yes, I know all too well, and worry about you because of it.

"Well, you haven't asked, but I'll tell you all about him anyway. His name is Oliver, and he's a total sweetheart. He tends to sleep a lot, but that's what happens when you get old, I guess."

Jeez, how old is this guy? At fifty-eight, her mother was still full of energy and always on the go. She couldn't imagine her with someone who slowed her roll. Suddenly, she realized her mother was still talking. What had she missed?

"His snoring is God awful and his eyesight is on the decline, but he seems to be able to hear just fine. Let's see, what else can I tell you? At bedtime, he hogs the covers, and we're both on meds for arthritis. I can't wait for you to meet him. I want to hear what you think of him."

"Mom, if he makes you happy, that's all that matters. It just seems so sudden."

"Yes well, at my age, there's no time to dilly dally. I'm going to send you a picture I took of us, just this morning. I'm sure you'll be able to see the mutual love in our eyes."

Whaa-aaa-t? Paige had never heard her mother talk like that about any love interest. Not that she would have expected her to talk about her father or stepfather. Paige wasn't sure she was ready for this. She heard the distinct ding of her phone alerting her to an incoming text message and found she couldn't resist the temptation to check out old lover boy.

Relieved by what she saw, Paige laughed wholeheartedly and hysterically. "Oh my God, Mom. He's handsome and dapper, not that I expected him to be any less than charming. Where in the world did you ever find a little cutie like that? As far as I recall, there was never more than one dog available for adoption on a good day in Juneau."

"There's a woman who moved here from Texas, hint-hint, imagine that. Anyway, she brought her passion for rehoming the unloved and unwanted with her here to Alaska. She works with a group that transports dogs all the way from South Texas, where I've heard there's an unfortunate surplus. You'll love the name of her rescue, it's Tiny Bubbas. One look and I knew he was destined to be mine."

Paige laughed. "I know that feeling, Mom. Listen, I'm gonna have some good news of my own to share soon. I promise as soon as I can tell you, I'll call. Meanwhile, send me all the pics and news you want. I might just get to see him sooner than you think."

"I hope so, honey. I'll keep my fingers crossed. I love you."

"I love you, too. More than mucho." With her childhood way of saying goodbye, Paige could've sworn she heard a tear escape her mother's eye.

***

Paige was in a great mood, ready to unwind and celebrate. But first, she went to share the news with her friend and set her free. She entered the room singing a happy song.

Dottie laughed. "I saw the news. I know why you're so happy you're singing. And believe it or not, I'm ready to go home."

"For real? You've got a bed!" Turner attempted to bounce on it, but the mattress failed to spring back and merely remained sunken in. "Nice or not, you've got cable TV, a shower—"

"I've about had all the spanking and slapping sounds a woman can handle in this no-tell motel." Dottie chuckled.

Turner laughed. "Are you serious?"

"Yeah, I'm serious. I never heard such moaning and groaning and carrying on, and all night long."

***

More than a week whizzed by before Paige found herself able to take a breath and a break. She was champing at the bit to spend some we;;-earned down time with Bobbi. Despite the fact that business was booming just in time for the summer tourist season, Bobbi always managed to find time for her. She'd arranged for them to have some time alone, before sharing the good news and celebrating with everyone.

When Bobbi's pickup pulled into the driveway, Paige saw her from the backyard. She was waiting for the flames below the grate to lower a bit, so she could grill the burgers and hotdogs. It was almost hot enough not to need the grill. She went through the house and invited Bobbi in through the front.

***

"Nice place you got here," I greeted her.

"It's not mine. I'm just renting, but it's cozy enough to feel like a place to call home. Come on in."

I stepped across the threshold and felt an immediate warmth wrap around me that had nothing to do with the room's comfortable temperature. Suddenly, a case of the jittery nerves kicked in. With no more business needs to use as an excuse, this get-together was purely for pleasure, a first date of sorts.

"Make yourself at home. Look around. Snoop a little." Paige laughed. "Oh, and don't mind Kona."

"Kona?"

"She's the coffee-colored canine wandering around here somewhere. She looks a little menacing, but don't let that fool you. She's a total love bug. I'll be back in a minute. I just want to check on the coals."

I accepted her invitation and looked around. What I found most interesting was the artwork and framed photographs that decorated most of the walls. I guessed, given the appearance, many of the stills were of Alaska's natural landscape. What a beautiful place it was. As I walked the hallway of the little, one-story bungalow, I noticed a room that was essentially an art studio. My eyes were particularly drawn to an unfinished canvas still sitting on the easel. *Why, could that be?* I decided I was wishfully painting myself into that unfinished picture, but it did appear to be a scene from the river walk.

I heard footsteps approach from behind.

"I didn't know you were an artist."

Paige laughed. "Clearly, you can see that I'm not. I paint because I like to, not because I'm any good at it."

"Interesting."

"How so?"

"Where do you get your inspiration?"

"Well, I don't jump out of bed in the middle of the night like I've heard some writers do to capture scenes before the dream fades from their memory. Painting is different, at least for me. It's a way to relax and express my emotions." She must have sensed my uncertainty. "Look at this one." She pulled a canvas out from behind a chair in the room. "It's just colors, but tell me, what do you think I was feeling when I painted it?"

I answered immediately, "Sadness?"

Paige smiled. "How do you know?"

"The colors. Blues, purples. I don't know, it's just a feeling I get when I look at it."

"Now, *that's* interesting. Much like a reader brings their personal experiences to the interpretation of a book, so too, does every person who appreciates a work of art. I don't know that, consciously, I was particularly unhappy when I painted this, but maybe I was."

I couldn't help but ask, "What about that one?" I pointed to the unfinished canvas and thought I saw a hint of a blush cross her face. "What were you feeling when you were painting this?"

Paige smiled. "I had just finished speaking with my mother on the phone. Although I was missing her, I remember thinking my painting was a way of keeping her close. More than anything, I think I was happy and hopeful."

"Tell me about it. What were you painting? *Y ¿quién es?*" I pointed to the image of a woman from the back as she walked off into the distance. I was pretty sure I knew who it was.

"I'm sure you recognize the stone bridges and familiar places of the river, unless my painted renditions are worse than I thought."

Not one to be easily dissuaded, I insisted, "¿Y la mujer allí? You've painted only the back of her. Is there some significance to that?"

"Only that I wasn't yet ready—Oh my God! The burgers! The dogs! I hope you like yours well done." With that, Paige went running out the back door. She grabbed a mitt and threw the grill's lid open. The smoke rolled out, but thankfully the food inside wasn't rendered completely inedible.

"I've always liked my dogs black, so no worries. Nothing a little ketchup and mustard and a lot of relish won't take care of."

"I'm such a domestic disaster."

"Oh, I don't know. I think you kinda fall in the cute category where grill sergeants are concerned. Your place is definitely a whole lot neater than mine."

"That's only because I'm never here. I even suck at being a dog mom. Poor Kona, I've resorted to putting in a doggie door and just bought a timed kibble drop." Paige looked at me in an indecipherable way. "You wanna move in with me?"

I nearly choked on the crunchy, just-this-side-of-black frank I'd just bit off. I had no idea if Paige was serious or not, so I had no clue how to respond. Although, I was pretty sure remaining wordless and requiring the Heimlich maneuver was not the way to go. I opted for humor. It usually served me well. "Well, it took us a while to get to the first date but it sounds like our U-Haul's engine is revving in overdrive."

Paige smiled but didn't seem too pleased with my response. "It was just a thought."

"Wait!" I cried. "Are you serious? I thought you were joking. I mean, you've seen my place. And you still want to share living space with me? Not sure what I could bring to the table."

"I like you Bobbi, and..." She wobbled her wimpy wiener woefully in my direction. "You're a damn good cook." She took a bite and made a face, setting that po' boy on her plate. "On second thought, maybe it's not such a good idea, after all. I'd pack on fifty pounds."

"On you, at worst a gain would result in some love handles. They sure ain't nothing for a woman-loving woman to complain about, but there's something I haven't told you yet."

"Uh-oh, why does this sound ominously like a kickoff to a true confession?"

I smiled hesitantly. "I could possibly be a package deal."

Paige let out a breath. "Oh, I know about Kacie. And frankly,"— Paige reached again for the sad hotdog—"pun intended, I think Kona would be happy to have a friend. The only thing that could make this funnier would be if Kacie were a dachshund." Paige laughed uproariously at her own joke.

"Funnier, huh? You're sure on a roll tonight, girlfriend. But it's not Kacie I'm talking about. Do you remember my mentioning Rachel?"

Paige pulled herself together and nodded.

"Well, long story short, she came to see me at Beta's the other day, only for a little while. It was long enough for me to find out that her mother has left town and left her to fend for herself."

"How old is she? Rachel, I mean."

"She's nineteen. An adult by law and old enough to be on her own, but not in my opinion. She's still in college. From what she told me, she never knows day to day, or night to night, whether she's going to have an empty couch at a friend's to try to get some sleep on."

Paige's smile felt gentle.

"She hasn't taken me up on my offer to live with me, yet, but I'm hoping she does. She's like a daughter to me and knowing what I know, well, it's tearing me apart."

"I can see how much you care about her. Just so you know, my offer still stands. I have three bedrooms here. She's welcome to come with you."

"Thank you. That means more to me than you'll ever know. Now, let's get a move on before the barrel babes race on by us."

I had finally talked Paige into taking the time to go with me to a rodeo. First, we had a few wardrobe malfunctions to make functional, so we headed to Cavender's.

***

"What about these?" I held out a pair of feather embroidered jeans for her approval.

Paige scrunched her face. "I don't know. Don't you think they have a little too much bling on the pockets?"

"Bling can be a good thing." I winked at her. "I like them, and I think they'll look fantastic on you. Be a sport and try them on. *¿Por favor?*"

"Okay, why not? Go ahead and add them to the pile."

The pile currently consisted of about six pair of jeans, all different brands and styles. I tossed them in the cart, and we moved on to the button-downs with a similar experience and outcome. My first fabulous find was a sheer, short-sleeved top that was a match made in heaven for the jeans I'd picked out. I didn't even pass that one by Paige for approval, simply snuck it into the bunch. After adding a few more tops, we were ready to hit the dressing room to try on the wardrobe, or so I thought.

Apparently, Paige was channeling her inner cowgirl. She stopped here, there, and everywhere, especially when we passed the boots on our way to the fitting stations at the back of the store.

"You can try those on out here, but we're cutting it close on time."

While admiring several others, Paige set aside a pair of very pricey boots. I approved. They were simple, yet stylish. I feared I'd regret this little fashion foray. The woman apparently had a taste for the expensive. Still, I smiled. "I think we're gonna have to let the hat and buckle selection wait until next time." I could've sworn I saw Paige frown.

"Okay. Let's go."

After almost another hour of sliding into tops and bottoms, checking hangs, fits, and feels, and the mirroring of each other's eyes, Paige decided to take home several of each. And, after paying by plastic, we hurried to remand all the bags to the back seat and headed for home, a word we both liked the sound of these days.

"*Hogar, dulce hogar,*" I proclaimed once we pulled to the curb out front. "I still can't believe you've been in Texas for six years and have never been to a rodeo of any kind."

"You've opened my eyes to the possibilities of so many new adventures. What can I say?" Paige teased me with her response.

"Just wait 'til you hear about the latest I have in mind."

"Hold that thought. I can't wait to hear all about it."

We quickly changed and readied ourselves for a night at the Tejas Rodeo in Bulverde. I caught Paige admiring the cord and western stitch design on her new footwear, as she fingered the pull straps of her boots and smiled. It was gonna be a great Saturday night.

Because we weren't too hungry, we shared a meal at the steakhouse on the rodeo grounds: some fried pickles and jalapeños, chicken fried steak, green chili mac and cheese, and a house salad. We even managed to squeeze in some of their incredible blackberry cobbler.

Afterward, we walked it off, or at least into a more comfortable place in our stomachs, by checking out the goods of the vendors outside the arena. While I was dying to get Paige on the mechanical bull, I knew now wasn't the best time. Maybe after the rodeo, once we'd had a chance to digest some of our dinner.

The Tejas Rodeo was billed as "The Greatest Show on Dirt," and I loved it. As small-town rodeos go, it was the best I'd known. The events kicked off at seven thirty, with the ride in of the flag-bearing horses, the singing of the national anthem, and the rodeo prayer. Next came mutton bustin', barrel racing, steer wrestling, tie down and team roping, and of course, bull riding.

"This is great," Paige yelled to be heard over the noise of the crowd and the announcer.

I smiled and slid a little closer on the stadium seat.

Our date night continued after the last of the livestock was returned to the corral and the venue owners invited us all to enjoy the all-night entertainment. Texas musician Aaron Watson was on stage, and when the words to *That Look* filled the interior of that weathered old dance hall I gave Paige my own look.

She leaned her head close to my ear and confessed, "I didn't know they made country songs like this."

"Yet another surprise from a woman who's been in Texas for six years." I shook my head. "*Increíble*. May I recommend a playlist for you? *'In Case You Didn't Know,' 'Only You Can Love Me This Way,' 'Strip It Down,' 'Till There's Nothing Left,'* by Brett Young, Keith Urban, Luke Bryan, and Cam, respectively."

Paige moistened her lips with her tongue. "I like how you did that. With the song titles I mean."

I winked at her. "You might be surprised. Much of today's country music could be classified as genre non-conforming. Try it, you might like it."

"I just might. After all"—Paige pulled her blouse away from her chest—"the clothes and accessories are already growing on me." She looked at me. "What do you say we get out of here and head home for a little private concert of our own?"

"A symphony in the sheets?"

"Now you're pillow talking."

We hurriedly made our way across the straw-strewn floor from neon to moonlight and toward the promise of a little romp in the hay.

***

"Now, about that latest adventure you have planned for us."

I smiled at Paige, shocked and pleased that she remembered.

"Although this"—she gestured to the sheets we were tangled in— "was definitely a new one for us, and certainly wonderful. Somehow I don't think it's what you had in mind." She reached for the pillows that had found their way to the footboard and sat on her knees in bed. It was a position she was unlikely to stay in for long.

"Are you sure you want to mix business with the pleasure we've just experienced?"

Paige smiled at me and hopped off. "Why don't you gather your thoughts while I trot off to the kitchen for some coffee. I have a feeling I'm gonna wanna be wide awake for this one."

I watched her sashay across the room and out the door and shook my head. Before I recovered from that sight, she was back.

"Here you go."

She handed me a mug filled to the brim. Black. Just the way I like it. She'd taken notice. She settled back into bed. This time resting her back against the pillows at the headboard.

"Well?"

Patience was not her best virtue.

"It's just a dream."

"Does this dream include me?"

"It does now. I mean it could."

"Bobbi, I've never known you to be so shy. I can't wait to hear what this dream's about."

"I've always wanted to do more with food. Maybe a different venue. Another menu."

"And ..." Paige took a sip of her coffee and stared.

"Lately I've been thinking about everything from a multi-star restaurant to a food truck. I can't make up my mind in which direction to go." I didn't know what to make of Paige's silence after I shared that, so I stammered to fill it. "I know. Now's not a good time. I'm just bouncing back from the hit we all just took. Anyway, it's always been just a dream."

Paige smiled and my heart warmed. It wasn't the coffee.

"Do you believe dreams can come true?"

"I do." I reached for her hand and took it in mine. "The best one already has. How could I possibly ask for more?"

Chapter Eighteen

ONCE FLYNN HAD BEEN caught, cuffed, and locked away, the rest of the pieces fell into place. A few of the letters of intent pointed the police to La China Poblana, and I got a little too much enjoyment out of watching Delgado get what he had coming to him. He was always so high and mighty. You know what they say, the higher they are, the farther they fall. I couldn't help but smile when they walked him down the steps in front of his restaurant. The photographers' flashes kept going off like crazy. Under other circumstances, the man would have primped and preened for the attention of the paparazzi. I couldn't wait to see the front page of the morning paper. I might just have to buy them all out. *Should I feel bad for feeling like I do? Nah. No way.*

Hoping for a light sentence, Delgado couldn't wait to rat out his buddy, Bigelow. Delgado didn't really know the man or exactly how he was involved, but one thing led to another. Phone records from Delgado led Turner to Bigelow. Not wanting to give the man a chance to remove or destroy any evidence, the police moved in swiftly with a search warrant. The rendering of his dream casino hung in a place of pride on the wall of the man's inner sanctum. His plans were ill-conceived. With the US Supreme Court's recent decision to let states make their own gambling decisions, the Texas governor's steadfast opposition to gaming practically ensures any and all casino bills that make it all the way to his mahogany desk in Austin will be killed. That fact continues to make the Kickapoo tribe of Eagle Pass happy.

After Delgado had been charged and taken away, the restaurant that he'd hoped to expand went on the market. Without hesitation, Paige and I seized the opportunity. After sharing my dream with her, she surprised me by saying that she'd been looking for an investment opportunity. Her stepfather left her with a little inheritance money. She'd been sitting on it, waiting for the right opportunity to come along. I sure hoped I could give her the return she deserved on her investment in me, in us.

As much as I hated to let Beta's go, we had bigger fish to fry. While we planned to keep the restaurant a little upscale, I didn't want to alienate my current clientele. The place was certainly big enough to divide in half, if we ultimately decided that's the way we wanted to go. How we could work that out and what that would mean exactly had yet to be determined, but one change had already been decided. La China Poblana would soon be called Garza's. I won that one, Turner's just didn't seem to do it for the place.

As for the cantina/restaurant that would soon be formerly known as Beta's, I found out more than the name would be changing. The new owners wanted to offer a different food choice. They told her they wanted to try Hawaiian. I had no sooner handed over the keys to my little cantina to Billie and Bety, than they excitedly shared their plans for the changes to the work-of-heart place. I was so happy for them, without even trying to blame freshly cut onions for my tears, I cried unabashedly.

"Imagine this," they told me. "C'mon. Close your eyes."

I did as I was told and smiled.

"We're gonna put sand out front where the outside seating is, under the entire Barefoot Patio Bar." Bety paused for dramatic effect there, and Billie took her turn at continuing to paint the perfect picture of their Hula Shack, the restaurant they were creating.

"Can you see the tiki torches and servers in grass skirts?"

"Will they be wearing coconut bras?" I laughed.

"I don't think your sister and our mother would let us go that far," both girls joined in response.

"Okay, you can open your eyes, but imagine this, Moco-Loco in the morning with fresh fruit and POG juices. We'll serve plate lunches of huli-huli chicken with mac salad and steamed white rice, just like they serve on the islands. We're thinking we'll carry over items for a lighter dinner selection, and add a few more choices, like Hawaiian quesadillas with pineapple, Canadian bacon and mozzarella. We're thinking about Kona-coffee-rubbed smoked brisket, maybe some shoyu chicken and coconut-crusted mahi, if we can get it."

Bety's descriptions of the food had me salivating, it sounded so delectably divine. Still, I had to ask, because I had the greed of a need to know, "And for dessert?"

"Ahhh. Pineapple-upside down and coconut cakes, a tropical fruit freeze—"

"If you need a taste tester, I'll take one for the team. Just let me know."

The girls laughed and Bety invited, "Of course, Tía. We'd be honored to have you help us create our menu, and we'll be happy to serve you in our taste kitchen. We'll let you know as soon as it opens."

"And," Billie shared more of their plans for the place, "for music, we'll play IZ, Eddie Tanaka, and Damian Awai. And for our weekend live nights, we've already been in touch with a local musician who plays the ukulele and just returned from a few years on the islands. You'll have to see, taste, and hear it to believe it."

I smiled, so proud and happy for them. "Just curious. Where'd you get the idea for Hawaiian?"

"Mom took us to Maui for our High School graduation. I've missed the food and wondered why it couldn't be made here. We came across a vendor at the Helotes Market Days, who inspired us. If he can do it under a little canopy once a month, we can do it here with a kitchen, full-time."

The girls were so excited. I hoped the public would be receptive. Ohana's had tried and failed with a similar cuisine on the north side of town. The coming change was already being advertised. I laughed as I reminded them, "Don't forget. You have me to thank for the interior rainbow motif already in place."

Life was good, and about to get so much better.

* * *

I had arranged a small gathering of merchants and friends to celebrate. Charlie, Di, Danny, Paul, Robbie, Dean, Bety, and Billie all came, as did others. In an attempt to be the hostess the occasion called for, I remained front and center, while Paige, sporting dark circles under her eyes and stifling a yawn, sauntered off in search of a collapsing place.

Charlie got the gossip ball rolling, "Thank God this nightmare is behind us. To think it all started as a scare tactic by a greedy gastronomer trying to move us out of here."

"Yeah well, I hope Sammy boy enjoys the three not-so-hots and the not-quite-a-cot he'll be getting in exchange," I chimed in.

As always, it was Di who reminded us of the worst tragedy of all. "Ay, those poor undeserving souls whose lives he so casually took away."

"You know, I heard that Flynn believed he was only giving them what they wanted, the drugs, and that they would have gotten them elsewhere anyway," Paul mentioned.

To which his partner, Danny, added, "Who knows? Maybe he was telling the truth when he claimed he didn't know he was offering a hyper-potent product. Maybe he didn't mean to kill anyone."

"Regardless, it was an illegal substance. I wonder where he got it, anyway."

"He's totally changed the holiday for years to come. Now, instead of Cinco de Mayo, it'll be Cinco de Die-o for all eternity."

"I think The Sentinel needs to own its role in that renaming."

"I'm just glad that life and business are finally getting back to normal."

"Of course I am too, but I have to admit I'm kinda disappointed that, once again, my hopes for a San Antonio River Walk casino have been dashed."

"Don't worry. It won't be long before someone will try again."

"Let's just hope whoever does will go about it in a different way."

I had lost track of who was saying what and went off in search of Paige, whose absence I felt like a giant void. I found her hunkered down, hiding in the kitchen, near the back door.

"*¿Qué haces aquí?* Wanting to be alone? Am I crashing your private party?'

"Never." Paige folded in half the section of the paper she'd been reading and handed it to me. Knowing I wouldn't have time to read it for a while, she filled me in with a brief synopsis. "It would appear that Kevin Jameson has, indeed, walked away with a nomination for the prestigious Pulitzer Prize. Read all about it. Ironically, it was the younger Flynn that clinched it for him. He opened the door by not writing the story of his father's fall from grace and handing it over to Jameson like he'd planned from the start."

Suddenly, from the dining room, shouts of "To Paige and Bobbi, our friends and saviors," and "To Garza and Turner, the new Cagney & Lacey," could be heard. We scrambled to get back to our guests, who were honoring us. Drinks were raised and toasts were made, and I noticed immediately that Paige was hiding something behind her back. After seeing me strain and stretch to see what it was, she laughed and handed a package to me.

"*¿Qué es esto?*"

"What's a party without a little present? Now, hurry and open it, before the rest see and feel bad for not having arrived with gifts in hand."

I hurriedly pulled the rolled item out of the paper bag and snapped it to its full size. It was a shirt, of the T variety. I read its personalized wording and laughed. "Where in the world did you get this?"

Paige's smile rivaled my own. "Tell me it wasn't made for you? That it doesn't fit you to a T?"

I pulled it over my head and turned for all to see, not that anyone else knew about my dirty little secret.

ALL I NEED TO KNOW ABOUT ~~LIFE~~ DEATH,
I LEARNED FROM WATCHING ID TV

"Hey. You laugh, but I just read about a nurse who saved a baby's life, thanks to information from a mystery novel she'd read. Truth is often stranger than fiction, and art imitates life. What can I say?"

Paige's expression changed at the reminder of that reality. "That's why I cringe at all the information so easily accessible online. All you have to do is watch a You Tube video to learn how to get away with murder and commit many lesser crimes. We have whole departments that dedicate their time to monitoring the most notorious sites, but there are simply too many of them, and more are created all the time."

"I often find myself wondering if there's *that* much more crime in the world these days, or if we're just much more aware of what's happening out there. We now have the news of the world at our fingertips via the global web."

Paige squinted her eyes at me. "You know, I think you may have missed your true calling. You'd make a hell of an investigator."

"Funny you should say that. *Había una vez,* I wanted nothing more than to be an FBI agent."

"A fed? Are you kidding me?"

"Cross my heart. When they built that nice new place over off Hausman, at University Heights, well I found out that ship had already sailed and left me behind."

Paige raised knitted eyebrows.

"I was too old to even apply."

"Definitely their loss." She shook her head.

I straightened myself to my full five foot two. "Maybe if I strut my stuff on the sidewalk where I can be seen sporting my new t-shirt, someone who can make a difference will look out the window, and they'll rethink their foolish, discriminatory hiring practices. The sails on my ship might catch a second wind."

"Couldn't hurt to try."

"Seriously, it's all good. I like being my own boss. And they can't stop me from solving a paperback mystery, or maybe lending an opinion to a local law enforcement officer willing to listen."

We smiled and clinked our glasses together.

"Would you be terribly disappointed if I were to say that I'm not sure I want to ever do this again, let alone do it over and over, day after day, for the rest of my wage-earning life? Constantly seeing the worst of people, I'm becoming so cynical and jaded. I want to go home at the end of my shift and feel good about myself, about what I'm doing. I want to make a positive difference in someone's life." Paige's confession surprised me.

I stayed quiet for a little while before finally asking, "What else would you do? Haven't you always been a *policia*?"

"I think the career chose me more than I chose it. I don't know, maybe I'm having an early mid-life crisis. Did you always know what you wanted to be?"

I chuckled. "I doubt the answer I gave my elementary school teachers all those years ago even remotely approximated what my adult reality has become. I'm happy with what I do. I feel good at the end of the day. I love making food, creating dishes I hope my customers will enjoy as creative culinary experiences. I like being a part of the many happy occasions people use food to celebrate. Think about all the special events that are catered or celebrated with *comida*. Not that I run that kind of place... Maybe what you need is a vacation, a change of scenery. If that doesn't do the trick, maybe a different position in a different unit."

We turned, as Joseph stood to make an announcement, "We'd like to invite you all to join us for a continuation of this celebration at the Bonham Exchange."

Billie and Bety were taking care of cleaning and closing, so Danny and the gang could shake off the memories of all that had happened in recent weeks with a night at their favorite dance club.

***

"Ladies and Gentlemen. Thank you for choosing to celebrate Pride at the Bonham Exchange. I'm DJ GAYbriel Ramos. In addition to our regularly scheduled programming, one of our own hometown heroes has an announcement she'd like to make. Paige, come on up here and join me on stage."

I looked at her and wondered what was happening, as the throng of party people clapped and whistled with voices and glasses raised. "A special request has been made for a special song with a special message for a special person, if you'll pardon my redundancy." Laughter was added to the mix of cheering, as the happy group gathered 'round. "I'm super tickled and pleased as punch to be a part of this dedication. Please make some noise with me. Give it up loud and proud for Paige and Bobbi." Our friends and family made the walls pulse and the floor vibrate with their increased response to his call.

Knowing nothing of the surprise that awaited me and assuming the DJ was merely referring to our roles in the apprehension of the San Antonio River Walk killer, my eyes got big and my mouth dropped open as Paige jumped off the stage. She made her way through the parting of the crowd and reached for my hand. Hundreds, if not thousands, of LGBTQ+ people became visual and auditory witnesses to the moment Sara Bareilles and Paige began singing, "I Choose You."

Paige looked at me and smiled. "*Quiero dedicarte esta canción, amor.*" She pulled me into her arms and together we slowly swayed.

"If I'm dreaming, please don't wake me." I looked at Paige through misty eyes. I hung on every word that Paige sang, as if she'd written them for me. When our song finished, the floor was reopened to everyone with Maluma's "Me Enamoré de Ti." Paige and I stayed on the floor and danced to the beat.

Afterward, we embraced, shared our first public kiss, and bid goodbye to our friends. Amid hoots and hollers, we walked away hand in hand. After a little meandering, we ultimately ended back on the river, where Paige noticed a subtle but definite change in my demeanor. Beta's transformation appeared to be well underway.

"Wow. Those girls sure don't waste any time, do they?"

I took note of the fact that my sign was gone and most of the exterior work had already been done. I walked to the door and peeped inside. The place had been gutted. I felt like I had too.

"Second thoughts? Regrets? Talk to me. What's on your mind?"

"Mostly I'm afraid. I am Beta. Beta's is...was...me and mine for many years."

"But now you're going to have Garza's, and it's literally across the river. It will be so much bigger, better than what you've let go."

"*Yo sé*. My head gets it, but my heart, that's an organ of a totally different nature."

Paige slid her hand into mine and we interlocked our fingers, as we made our way to what would be our joint venture on the other side. "Not much going on here. The ink on the contract we signed is barely even dry. Bobbi, are you sure you want to do this? It's not too late to change your mind. Why don't you take some time to think about it? I'd say, given all your efforts in solving these crimes, you've earned yourself a vacation."

"Sounds lovely, but we just bought a new restaurant. How can we afford to leave now?"

"It'll take a few weeks for the renovations to even begin. This is likely our one and only opportunity for a getaway, and I have just the place. You said you want to get to know me better. Everyone's life story has roots in the environment in which they were raised. I've got a little something for you that I hope will get you excited for the experience." She reached into her bag and pulled out a book. "No, it's neither the *Kama Sutra* nor *The Joy of Sex*, so lock your disappointment in a chastity belt."

I smiled. "Guilty as charged. All I know about Alaska I learned from *The Call of the Wild* and *Ice Road Truckers*. Although, I have heard it's the final frontier for criminals who want to hide away."

Paige shook her head and frowned. "It gets such a bad rap for such a beautiful place."

I looked at the book. "A ver...what do we have here? *If You Lived Here, I'd Know Your Name* by Heather Lende."

"Welcome to a preview in prose of what it's like to live in small-town coastal Alaska."

"I can't wait to read it."

***

I had to put the book aside and wait to read it, because Paige insisted we form our fledgling family and feather our nest, as soon as possible. We cleaned out closets, tossed the unneeded, packed the rest, and reminisced throughout the process. It wasn't until we carried the last box off the moving van's ramp and into the house formerly known only as Paige's, that I was able to sit for a bit. "Did I ever tell you that I often dream of houses?" I asked.

"God, please tell me you're not thinking of going out of the restaurant business and into real estate? At least not right now. I don't think I can take on any more change at the moment."

"No, silly. I had another one last night. I'd forgotten about it until just now."

"Those into interpreting dreams say that houses are symbolic of yourself. If you dream, for example, someone is breaking into your house and you're afraid, maybe someone is trying to get close to you and that scares you."

I twisted my mouth, holding my words for a moment before I released them. "Details of my dreams tend to quickly vanish once I awaken, so I usually keep a journal. As a matter of fact, because I didn't reach for my notebook, all I can remember from last night's is that there was a big storm, with lots of wind. Trees were uprooted, and it was dark. I walked outside and saw a man at a truck just outside the garage, so close. I had no sooner battened that hatch, than a bolt of lightning illuminated another man standing in the backyard."

"Sounds like more of a nightmare than a dream. If it makes you feel any better, I not only keep a gun in the nightstand, but I have deadbolts on all the doors. And I pay a pretty penny for home monitoring and security."

"Well, that does make me feel a little better, especially about leaving Rachel here, all alone, when we go away."

Rachel had been listening from not so afar and offered a solution, "You can always take me along."

We both laughed.

"I'm afraid not this time. It's almost like a honeymoon for us," I quickly explained.

"Sans the wedding." Paige added with lips pressed together in a halfhearted smile. "Always the bridesmaid."

"It could be worse. Better the bridesmaid than the handmaid in a world where women aren't allowed to read and must lay on their backs and pray for pregnancy."

"My dear Bobbi. All this time, I thought all you did was watch TV."

"Just what exactly did you think was inside all of the heaviest boxes we just unloaded? Last count, I had over seven hundred books at home."

"Sounds like the last of the spare rooms will have to be a library."

***

Later that evening, when we'd lost the war to tired and aching muscles that rendered us too exhausted to do any more, we attempted a secret rendezvous. We had only enough energy to lay passively next to one another in bed.

Older houses, while undeniably in possession of a certain charm many newer dwellings lack, cannot compete with modern hardware. Their parts, like the pops of an elderly human's joints, squeak their own moans and groans by way of doors that scream orgasmically on worn hinges. We found this out the embarrassing way when metal in need of a little lubrication announced our uninhibited intention for some nocturnal naughtiness.

"Moms," Rachel's voice rang loud and clear from across the expanse of the house. "You know you guys don't have to go sneaking around like teenagers. It's not like I don't know you're sleeping together." She giggled uncontrollably, until the double click of a closing and locking door soon muffled the sound of her laughter. Other noises, ultimately, silenced it completely.

Chapter Nineteen

"FINALLY. THERE'S SOME GOOD news in the paper," Paige announced over breakfast.

"*Sí*, what's that?" I slid two over-medium eggs onto her plate next to some home fries and sausage.

"Michael Flynn's wife, likely soon to be ex, has donated some mega money to the city and earmarked it for the homeless."

"I guess it's her way of trying to make reparations. I can't imagine the torment she must be going through, in every way imaginable."

Suddenly, Paige's eyes grew big. I could tell when she was getting excited.

"This could be it!" She bent the top half of the open paper toward her, so she could peer over it.

"Be what?" I tried to entice her to spill it. Her thoughts, not the hot sauce she held ready to pour.

"The answer to my professional dilemma."

I raised my eyebrows and repeatedly nodded my head, encouraging her to keep talking.

"Other than crossing paths with you and having the excuse to get together with you time and again, and I mean *waaaay* other than..." Paige reached across the table to take my hand. "The only time I felt even remotely good during this whole ordeal was when I helped Dottie and volunteered in the soup kitchen and community outreach to the homeless."

I leaned in to better focus and listen.

"What if I found a way to transition to a unit of homeless liaison officers, or to be the first if a unit doesn't already exist."

"What would that mean? *¿Qué harías?*" The excitement was contagious. I was now feeling it, too.

"Well, I would think they'd partner with mental health and other support organizations to provide homeless individuals with opportunities to get off the streets and into permanent housing. RISE, the youth center, is part of St. Benedict's. They serve those between the ages of eighteen and twenty-four. Half of Bexar County homeless youth identify as LGBTQ+ and are a vulnerable population. Many are kicked out of their homes, abused at shelters, and suffer from mental health and substance abuse challenges. I'm sure it would involve a close partnership with caseworkers who help with counseling, education, life issues, relationship skills, finding jobs and housing, you name it."

"And why, or how, in addition to all of the social services organizations you've just mentioned, are the police involved?"

"The homeless are both an easy target for crimes, as we've just witnessed, and often commit crimes themselves, either to obtain life's necessities or to abuse illegal substances. Burglary, robbery, and shoplifting are often crimes of poverty. That's definitely a category the homeless fall into. By focusing on that part of the population, hopefully we could help eliminate a portion of the crimes committed against and by them. It's a win-win for everyone."

***

Paige demanded I experience flight in a small, blade-spinning aircraft.

"Don't look at me like that. You can't come to Alaska and not fly in a floatplane."

It wasn't that bad. I only changed a few shades of green and managed to keep the fry bread inside me, as the pilot soared toward the snow-capped mountains, only to bank hard at the last minute and zoom downward to a water strip. We air toured Pack Creek for twenty-five minutes, in search of bears. The pilot guaranteed a sighting. I wasn't sure how I felt about that. Never a fan of zoos or circuses, I wanted more than anything to see one in the wild, yet I was terrified.

To say it was an exhilarating experience doesn't do it justice. It's certainly one I'll never forget. We listened to our guide describe Admiralty Island and its world-ranking bear population. We donned the rubber waders our guide provided and walked a brief hike. We rounded a bend and gasped at the sight of a small group of grizzlies about thirty feet ahead. They were in the creek, chasing wild salmon. As we sat on the pebbled shore and watched the show, I happened to glance at the shirt I'd put on and nudged Paige to get her attention.

"What color would you say this is?" I pulled my polo away from my body a little, so she'd know it was my pale, pink-orange-coral colored shirt I was talking about.

She seemed confused as to why I'd be thinking about what I was wearing at that particular once-in-a-lifetime moment but humored me all the same. "Uh, salmon?"

"That's what I was afraid of."

She couldn't help but break out in a broad smile. "I don't think you have to worry. They're far more interested in living, moving things." Her eyes drifted back to the shaggy, menacing, fish-loving creatures.

I'm not sure she heard when I mumbled, "Thank God I'm sitting still and wearing a bra."

***

Thankfully, by the time we made it to Momma Turner's home sweet home, I'd regained my land legs. Mrs. Turner, a.k.a. Alicia, had been waiting anxiously for our arrival, evident in the fact that she was already on the porch when we got there. Paige ran to her like I imagined she did when she was a little girl. Only this time, *she* was the one who nearly swung her mother off the ground. Tears of joy were flowing freely at this mother and child reunion. There was so much two-way love evident in their long-lasting embrace.

Finally, mother and daughter moved back and away from each other. Alicia opened her arms to me, immediately encircling me with the same expression of love. The feeling was so strong, I cried from joy and happiness...such intense emotion.

Before letting me go, Alicia whispered in my ear, "You must be special. She's never brought anyone home before. I just thought you should know."

"Mom. What are you telling her? Bobbi, get over here in my safe zone, now," Paige cried out.

My smile couldn't have been any bigger. I felt like I was the one who was coming home. The house was so lovely and warm, so inviting and cozy. And the woman who gave birth to Paige was beyond belief. As you might imagine a home decorated by a librarian might be, it was filled, wall to wall, with more books than the mind could count or the eyes could see.

"I'm so happy to have you both here. I hope you'll find a little time in your itinerary to include me. I don't want to intrude, but I so want to take advantage of all the time I can get with you. It's such a precious commodity. One I don't get near enough of these days."

"Mom, you know you're welcome to come with us wherever we go. Now get your stuff, and let's get a move on. I'm starving." Paige pointed to me. "This woman is a foodie of the finest form. I've already decided where I want to take her and what I want to get her to try. Who knows? Maybe some of it will find its way to a menu back in Texas, one day."

***

My first Alaskan meal was called a sled dog and consisted of reindeer sausage wrapped in sourdough bread.

"You've all of a sudden gotten quiet." A smile tugged hard at Paige's full and sensuous lips.

"*Estoy comiendo. ¿Qué quieres que haga?* Should I chew with my mouth open so I can talk?"

Paige laughed. "You're doing more than eating and you know it. I've seen that look on your face many times. I'll bet you a dozen home-cooked meals; you're thinking about your food truck fantasy and scheming how you can put this little culinary gem on the grill on wheels."

"First of all, missy, I'm not so sure your bet is one I'd like to win. Maybe, if you change it to restaurant meals instead of home-cooked by you..." I smiled. "How is it that you already know me so well? We're like an old married couple."

As soon as those words left my mouth and entered the universe, I found myself fearing what Paige might suggest next. I hurried to fill the ensuing silence. "What do you think? Is there any way possible we can get *reno* meat anywhere near San Antonio? More importantly, do you think anyone would even try it?"

"In for a peso in for a pound. I say, why not go all the way? Instead of the usual beef, use caribou in the chili on the dogs." Paige paused there before expelling a long and loving sigh. "God help us with the aftermath of a lunch at Tracy's King Crab Shack."

I laughed. "I did see Tracy had some pretty cool choices for her bottled brews, Hopothermia and Icy Bay IPA. I can't wait to see what we could craft with our combined imaginations."

"How about throwing a few burgers on the fire and calling one Angus Borealis?"

"Now you're talking. Welcome to my world."

After taking a Fjord Express up the Chilkoot Inlet to Haines, I insisted on seeing how well reality had been depicted in the book, and we set off for a walk into the wild. Along the way, I marveled at the sights and sounds of species I'd only ever seen in pictures and on TV. By far, I found the moose to be the most amazing. I hadn't realized how big a life-sized Bullwinkle would be. They are enormous and majestic creatures.

For her part, Paige delighted in my reaction to this place farther away than what I'd ever known. "You know, we can always sell the restaurant. I don't think we'd have any trouble finding a buyer now that life on the river is back to normal. I mean in case you think you'd like to staycation here permanently."

I smiled. "I don't know that I'm ready to commit to that, yet. Maybe by the end of our trip. As for the restaurant, I guess so. I mean, after all, it wasn't all that long ago that certain men were willing to kill for the opportunity to get their hands on some primo San Antonio River Walk property."

Paige looked at me, her eyebrows raised.

"*Lo siento*. You know how I get when I'm nervous. But, I think this place could grow on me, and I *really* like your mom."

"She is pretty special. You know, she likes you too."

"I kinda got that impression."

***

Day two required an early rise. Paige had arranged a whale-watching trip. We were fortunate to chance upon a pod of orca so close the captain had to cut the engines. It was amazing.

"Wow. Unbelievable. You know, I boycott Sea World. I can't stand to see dorsal fins slumped over in sadness. Whales belong in the wild, just like this. They shouldn't be held hostage to the whims of human entertainment." I looked at Paige with my heart on my sleeve and in my eyes. "Thank you so much for sharing this with me. I can't imagine why you ever wanted to leave this place."

"Well, let's see if you change your mind and tune after our next stop at the frosty surface of the Mendenhall Glacier. You can get a tiny feel for what winter is like here. If you're feeling particularly adventuresome, we can hike through the Tongass National Forest and go into the half-mile wide caves for a little under-ice exploration."

***

"I have a confession to make. Before I knew where you were bringing me, I'd envisioned a vacation to a much more tropical destination. One with white sandy beaches, relaxing ocean waves, refreshing umbrella drinks—"

"And maybe women in bikinis?"

"Well, maybe just one in particular."

The words had no sooner made it out of my mouth, before Paige unzipped her polar fleece outer garments to reveal, well, use your imagination.

Doubling over with laughter, the roar of my hilarity nearly caused the glacier to calve.

"I c-c-couldn't possibly ask you to f-f-forsake everything, but you'd b-b-better take a nice, long look, 'cause this is a l-l-limited t-t-time offer. S-s-sorry, but a polar bear p-p-plunge is now off the t-t-table."

Pulling myself together, I insisted, "Please put your clothes back on or we'll spend the rest of our arctic vacation in a hospital. Let's save that fantasy fulfillment for another time."

***

Day three took us to Gold Creek for a little mining experience and salmon bake. Roasted over a wood fire with a brown sugar glaze, the entrée was absolutely delicious. On our return trip from another full day's experience, we happened upon a field full of majestic bald eagles. Maybe it was a routine sight to those who lived in such a place, but my mouth fell open in awe before the big birds, our country's symbol of freedom.

"It's so incredibly beautiful here," I remarked to Paige.

"I concur. I guess I stopped seeing it when I was here, but now that I'm back after having been away, I can honestly say it is pretty amazing. If you're up to the gills in seafood, we can always grab a steak, Italian, or some chicken."

"Are you kidding me? This is the best, freshest seafood I've ever had. I rarely eat it at home because, well because it's not like this. Straight outta Alaskan waters. Baked, fried, broiled, seared, salmon, crab, halibut, it's all been delicious."

So, off to Twisted Fish Company we went. I chose broiled wild salmon with a side of mandarin-mango salsa, while Paige ordered the halibut *picatta*, lightly seasoned and sautéed in a lemon and caper wine sauce over linguine *aglio*. Alicia went for the halibut and chips. We shared sides of green beans and scalloped potatoes and a basket of herb-and-cheese knotted bread.

"Dare I ask what's on the agenda for tomorrow?" I played it risky and soon discovered that no trip to Alaska is complete without a little fishing expedition. Not hook, line, and sinker, but a little dip netting for sockeye salmon in the Kenai River, before heading out into deeper waters for some drift gillnetting. I was shown how nets are lowered into the water for varying durations from a few minutes to an entire day, depending on the weather and the number of fish that become entangled in the ropes. When the floats along the top of the net begin to shimmy and shake, the net is pulled out of the water and the fish are dumped into the boat's hold. Once the net is reset, the process repeats as many times and for as long as you want it to take.

* * *

The sun set as we pulled in the last net for the day.

I was looking forward to a calm, quiet, uneventful evening. We were scheduled to fly back to Texas in the morning.

Paige and I looked at each other at the same moment, with the same expression of shock and dismay after our eyes caught sight of something I thought we couldn't possibly be seeing. In tandem, we bent for a closer look.

"*Por el amor de Dios*, it can't be."

But it was, and we both knew it. We just couldn't believe it.

There, entangled beneath a substantial haul of fish, was what appeared to be the arm of a person. I turned away before I could see if other body parts were attached to it.

"Hold the net," Paige called to the captain/deckhand we'd hired to woman the ship. The motor that pulled the giant net was stalled. Indeed, the rest of the woman's anatomy joined her arm. Although bloated, it didn't appear she'd been in the water too long. The salt may have helped to preserve the body. I chanced a look at the woman's face. Her eyes bulged open, and the expression of her mouth seemed to be begging us to figure out what had happened to her. Like it or not, I knew we were about to embark on an extended and at least semiworking vacation.

To be continued …

About Toni Draper

Toni Draper was born and lived most of her life in the Mid-Atlantic state of Maryland. These days, she calls home a cozy casita on a two-acre sprawl deep in the heart of Texas. She shares her rancher with her wife and their current pack of perros: Kona, Juneau, Tucker, and Ellie. With an undying passion for the rescue of senior and special needs canines, she has opened her heart and home to many *under*dogs over the years, and likes to immortalize them via *nods* on her pages. When not reading, writing, or vacationing, she teaches - and is thankful for a degreed and certified ability to read, speak, and write Spanish, a language that is not her first, yet somehow *siempre* seems to find its way into her writing. Her debut novel WILDFIRE, a second-chance lesbian romance, was published in July 2021.

To Connect with Toni

Email
Webpage – https://tonirdraper.com
Twitter – tonirdraper
Instagram – tonirdraper
Facebook - https://www.facebook.com/toni.draper.9083

Note to Readers:

Thank you for reading a book from Desert Palm Press. We have made every effort to edit this book. However, typos do slip in. If you find an error in the text, please email lee@desertpalmpress.com so the issue can be corrected.

We appreciate you as a reader and want to ensure you enjoy the reading process. We would like you to consider posting a review on your preferred media sites and/or your blog or website.

For more information on upcoming releases, author interviews, contests, giveaways and more, please sign up for our newsletter and visit us as at Desert Palm Press: www.desertpalmpress.com and "Like" us on Facebook: Desert Palm Press.

Bright Blessings